Dear Guest,

In *The Greatest Player Who Never Lived*, Michael ⟨...⟩ ls a captivating tale that combines the suspense of a murder mystery with the pursuit of the virtues in life we would all hope to share.

The pivotal character in the story, Beau Stedman, is a potential world-class golfer who, at the age of 19, is wrongly accused of committing murder. Stedman is forced to go underground, but thanks to world-famous golfer and old friend Bobby Jones, he perseveres. Their strong friendship sees Stedman through the toughest times, and as he put it, "when I couldn't fit in the real world, (Jones) made another world for me."

What got Stedman through his worst days? In his own words, it was the simple pleasure of "hitting the ball in the middle of the club face...or seeing it go where you want it to go." While you are here at Grayhawk, we hope you enjoy these simple pleasures as well.

Evidenced by his refusal to let bitterness or regret steal his energy, and his commitment to "answer every one of life's bogeys with a birdie," we're confident that Beau would agree with us when we say, "The game of life is in the flight."

Sincerely,

Gregg Tryhus
President

Del Cochran
Captain o' the Club

THE GREATEST PLAYER
WHO NEVER LIVED

A Golf Story

J. MICHAEL VERON

Sleeping Bear Press

PUBLISHER

Sleeping Bear Press
310 North Main
P.O. Box 20
Chelsea, Michigan 48118
www.sleepingbearpress.com

Printed and bound in The United States.
10 9 8 7 6 5 4 3 2

Library of Congress Cataloging-in-Publication Data
Veron, Michael
The greatest player who never lived: a golf story / Michael
Veron.
p. cm.
ISBN 1-886947-89-9
1. Golfers--Fiction. 2. Golf--Fiction. I. Title.

PS3572.E763 G7 2000
813'.6--dc21

For Melinda

Preface

I first met Charley Hunter when he was a student editor of the *Tulane Law Review* and was assigned to edit an article I had written. He was a pleasure to work with and offered numerous helpful suggestions that greatly improved my essay on conflicts of interest in class action litigation.

While we were working together, Charley learned about my interest in golf and shared with me his discoveries about Beau Stedman. After my law review article was published, we stayed in touch, and I followed with great interest his efforts to bring Stedman's story to light.

Charley eventually asked me to tell that story, and this book is the result. I am grateful that he allowed me to be his amanuensis.

Charley and I have stayed in touch since I completed this book. In fact, he called not long ago to inform me that he had won his first big case. It appears that he is headed for a sterling career as a trial lawyer. I suspect that we will hear more from him in the future.

Acknowledgments

I was introduced to Bo Links indirectly several years ago when I purchased *Follow the Wind*, a wonderful golf novel he wrote in 1995. I thoroughly enjoyed reading Bo's tale of a young man who meets Ben Hogan and other greats of golf at a mythical club he discovers upon walking through a fog-filled portal in Lincoln Park Golf Course in San Francisco.

Our formal introduction came a short time later, when the United States Golf Association invited us to share a podium to discuss legal issues in golf at an annual meeting of the Golf Course Superintendents Association of America. We soon discovered that we had much in common (one of the USGA staffers said we were so much alike that we could have been twins separated at birth), and Bo encouraged me to share Charley Hunter's story with others. He also read the first draft of my manuscript and made many suggestions, all of which I found helpful. More than anyone, Bo made it possible for me to join the fraternity of golf writers, and it's the best club I've ever belonged to. I am deeply grateful for his support and encouragement.

Another individual who played a big role in making Charley's story a reality is my faithful secretary Marilyn Haile, who transcribed the initial draft of this book from my dictation. She then helped me with revisions by teaching me to understand the mysteries of word-processing software. Through it all, Marilyn never complained that this was over and above her usual duties, and Charley and I are both grateful to her for helping me get his story right.

Of course, none of this would ever have happened without the support of my family, who made it possible for me to have sufficient "quiet time" to get Charley's story in print. They shared Charley's belief that Beau Stedman deserved his rightful place in golf history, and they were willing to give up time with me in order to see it done. They know how much I love them and that I will make it up to them.

Obviously, I am indebted to Brian Lewis, Lynne Johnson, Jennifer Lundahl, Danny Freels, Adam Rifenberick, Karmel Bycraft, and everyone else at Sleeping Bear Press, Inc., for their faith in me. I thought very carefully about whom I should entrust with Beau Stedman's story, and they were the first and only ones to whom I submitted the manuscript of this book. I am pleased and proud to be with a publisher that has contributed so much to golf literature.

Finally, my thanks to my friends and golfing buddies, particularly Robert Dampf and Dr. Charles Horn, who encouraged and challenged me to get Beau Stedman the recognition he deserved. There's no telling how much of this book was inspired by the tales we've spun while walking the fairways together on Saturday mornings.

Chapter 1

THE FUNNY THING IS, I didn't even much like golf at the time. Oh, I had played often enough that I could keep up in a social game. I guess you could say that I played well enough not to embarrass myself but not so well as to embarrass anyone else, either.

What my game really lacked was not so much talent but passion. My good shots didn't inspire poetry, and my bad shots didn't cause the searing pain that appeared to inflict those who took the game more seriously. I never broke a club, for instance. It's not that breaking clubs is something I would have been proud of, but bad golf has to hurt you enough at some point or you won't care to get better. I clearly didn't care enough.

Suffice it to say that the inner mysteries of the game had not yet revealed themselves to me at the time. Although I didn't know it then, they were looming on the horizon, however, and my days of being content just nibbling on the outer edges of the game were drawing to an end.

The whole thing started on an otherwise unremarkable Monday morning in Atlanta. I had just finished my first year of law school at Tulane and had done the Hunter clan proud, finishing third in the class. This qualified me for an invitation to the law review and with it a good number of offers of summer employment with various law firms around the country.

Making law review was a lot like making the homecoming court (or so I imagine). Each day, suitors sent notes through the mail, introducing their firms to the "top ten percenters" and telling us what a wonderful summer was in store for us if we would accept a date with them. The rush actually started after the first semester, when our first law school grades were announced and it became evident who the supposed "stars" of the class were.

After briefly considering a couple of firms in New Orleans and one in San Francisco (where I couldn't afford the housing), I finally settled on Butler & Yates in Atlanta. It wasn't that hard a decision. For one thing, I wanted to get out of New Orleans for the summer and at least get above sea level where the air wasn't so dense and sticky. Being from Birmingham, I knew enough about Atlanta to be comfortable with it. Also, I was a Braves fan, and the firm had good seats they promised we could use.

The firm was about the right size, too. It was what I called my Goldilocks firm — not too big, not too small, but just right.

It might take me the entire summer, but I figured that I would know just about everyone by the time I left for my second year of law school.

Butler & Yates was a fairly old firm, but the lawyers who recruited law clerks were young and were more inclined to talk about the firm's website than about its traditions. That's why I didn't know until that Monday morning, my first day on the job, that Bobby Jones had been a partner in the firm.

That's right. That Bobby Jones. The man many call the greatest golfer who ever lived. I knew enough about him when I learned about it to be impressed, but that was about it. Certainly not as much as I know now. But I'm getting ahead of myself. The subject of Bobby Jones actually came up as a way of introducing me to my first project.

You have to understand, there's not much first-year law students can do as summer clerks. The first year of law school doesn't cover much more than basic concepts of torts, contracts, criminal law, and procedure. As a result, first-year clerks are more window dressing than anything else. They can't do more than the simplest research assignments. Maybe shuffle some papers or organize files. Run to the courthouse to file pleadings. Catalog documents being produced during discovery. That's about it.

For this reason, law firms don't hire first-year students for what they can do; the real reason they hire them is to get a foot in the door to recruit them after graduation. Thus, in reality, the salaries paid first-year clerks are really seed money. So, when Charles Hunter showed up for work that first summer after just one year of law school at Tulane, the partners at the firm weren't expecting much.

Of course, no one admits this. They're much too polite for that. Besides, there's no need to risk offending the recruits with such candor. Unless they have IQs lower than mayonnaise, they'll find out soon enough on their own.

At least that's what happened in my case. It didn't take me long to realize how little I knew. I just watched what the lawyers were doing and saw that it was over my head.

So when the firm went looking for ways to keep the otherwise worthless first-year clerks busy, someone came up with the bright idea that one of us could be kept occupied the entire summer cataloging what was left of Jones's files. Not that they expected to come up with anything sexy; Jones had written several books during his lifetime sharing the great events of his life and his secrets about golf. When he died in 1971, his family and friends inherited a treasure trove of trophies, medals, and other memorabilia.

The only things left at the firm were his legal files, which were protected from publication by the attorney-client privilege. Besides, they belonged to the law firm and its clients and could not be inherited by Jones's survivors. At any rate, the public never really cared all that much about Jones's legal work. It was his golf that interested them.

Over the years, most of the files became scattered as other lawyers completed work that had been in progress when Jones withdrew from practice. Many clients, conscious of the value of anything with Jones's signature, wanted their files and so took them from the firm.

Fred Nathan, the partner who seemed most responsible for keeping us busy, tried to make my assignment sound important, but I saw it for what it was. Not that I minded; it would keep me busy, and it was not something I was likely to screw up. Just the ticket to get me invited back next summer — if I wanted to return. That, it seemed to me, would depend mostly on the number of Braves games I was invited to attend.

Nathan was an interesting guy. He was reputed to be a genius at securities law and had allegedly spent virtually his entire career drafting, editing, and reading the fine-printed disclaimers contained in prospectuses (or could that be prospecti?) circulated as part of initial public offerings of stock. Nathan certainly gave the appearance of having suffered severe eyestrain for his labors; he wore glasses so thick they reminded me of Roy Orbison. If they had been tinted green, I would have expected to see the name of the town in which Coca Cola was bottled written in a circular fashion along their outer edges.

At any rate, Jones's remaining files had been put in boxes that were stacked in a single room just off to the side of the library. The room had no windows and bare walls that needed fresh paint — hardly a shrine to the man who retired at age 28 after winning the four major championships of his time all in one year. The drab, brown carpeting suggested that the room had once been used as an office or for conferences, but not recently. There was a small table with a computer. It had been loaded with a software program designed to organize document production in litigation. The indexing system was simple enough. I could easily use it.

In the beginning, the work seemed pretty mundane. Jones had an office practice, which was less glamorous to me than litigation. Many of the files consisted of title searches, incorporations, and wills. Aside from his name, there was nothing there to distinguish Jones from any other good lawyer who had competently performed these same services.

The other clerks thought I was nuts when I complained, especially Ken Cheatwood. Of all the law clerks, he was the most instantly likeable. Cheatwood had just completed his first year at Emory (which just appeared to be the law school that Jones was attending when he passed the bar). Before that, he played college golf at Oklahoma State and then spent several years bouncing around the mini-tours. After deciding, in his words, that "you can't play games all your life," he took the LSAT and surprised himself by scoring in the 97th percentile.

Because he was originally from Georgia, he applied to Emory and was accepted largely on the strength of his LSAT score and despite what he described as a decidedly indifferent college transcript.

It seemed odd to me that Cheatwood claimed to have been a poor student in college. He was not only bright but intellectually curious as well. Not many players amass a collection of golf literature like he had; that was usually something golf historians and librarians did.

After I had gotten to know him well enough to know it wouldn't offend him, I asked him about it.

"I still had a lotta growing up to do when I was in college.

Collecting books was fun because it was about golf. More do it than you realize. From what I understand, Ben Crenshaw has an awesome golf library. Besides, studying economics or political science was too much like work. I figured I was gonna be on tour in a couple of years anyway, so what was the point? So I basically hung out at the fraternity house or with the golf team. Mostly just played gin rummy and drank beer."

Because of his background, Cheatwood had also grown up with the Jones mystique and chided me for not appreciating my good fortune.

"For God's sake, Charley, don't you realize what you have?"

I didn't bother to respond because I knew he was about to answer his own question.

"You're getting an inside look at the greatest player who ever lived. He won every major championship of his day. Then he won 'em all in one year. That's when they first called it 'The Grand Slam.' He beat the greatest pros in the world, and he was an amateur. When he played overseas, the British bookies made him even-money against the field."

"I haven't found much of that so far," I protested weakly.

"How much have you looked at?"

"I've only gotten through a couple of boxes," I admitted. "There must be a hundred or more."

Cheatwood shook his head. "You're looking at history, Charley. There's bound to be some great golf stuff in there somewhere."

Cheatwood's prophecy came true less than a week later. That's when I first learned about Beau Stedman.

Chapter 2

AFTER ALMOST TWO weeks of indexing half-century-old real estate transactions and what-not, I was thrilled to come across a box of files containing something different. At last, here were some files that were more of a personal nature, even though they were set up to look like law firm files. This may have explained how they escaped the attention of Jones's survivors, who had long since taken possession of all of his personal papers and correspondence.

They weren't as neatly organized as the other files, however. In fact, after looking through them for the better part of the day, I began to believe that maybe Jones himself maintained these files rather than a secretary. Lawyers are notoriously poor file managers, and from the looks of things a lawyer had put this file together. Some of the file labels seemed unrelated to the contents. The more I read, the more curious I became.

What were these files, anyway?

Many of them contained old press clippings of tournaments in which Jones competed. By all accounts, however, Jones was reputed to be self-effacing. He was not likely to retain his own press clippings.

My curiosity inspired, I began to read each clipping. There is something about reading contemporaneous accounts from the past that makes the events come alive in ways that historians cannot recapture. The style of the day comes through in the writing. Sitting there in my little office, I had my own private window into the early part of the century.

It was apparent from reading these accounts that Jones was an extraordinary player. He entered few tournaments outside of golf's major championships, which at the time were the U.S. Open, the U.S. Amateur, the British Open, and the British Amateur. In the Opens, he was competing against professionals who played year-round. Yet Jones remained an amateur who practiced law full-time and really only played golf from April to October.

Apparently, Jones played little if any golf over the winter. Each spring, like so many other amateur golfers, he would dust off his clubs and begin to prepare for the coming golf season. The only difference was that, while other amateurs prepared for their member-guest or club championship, Jones was warming up for a summer of world-class competition.

He often didn't play in a single tournament until the old Southeastern Open in Atlanta, which was held only a few weeks before the U.S. Open. Other than that, he might play in the Southern Amateur or one or two other regional events, but that was his only competition before playing in the U.S. Open, the U.S. Amateur, the British Open, and (schedule permitting) the British Amateur. In view of how little competitive golf Jones actually played prior to these major championships, his sterling record in the major championships becomes all the more remarkable. Even so, Jones was considered to be as likely as not to win virtually every time he teed it up.

Jones was a prodigy who first came to prominence by playing in the U.S. Amateur in 1916 when he was only 14 years old. Throughout his teen years he compiled a remarkable record, winning numerous amateur championships. And he did so while studying engineering at Georgia Tech, English literature at Harvard, and law at Emory. After several near-misses — and after learning to curb a temper that often betrayed him in competition — Jones followed a second-place finish, one stroke behind Gene Sarazen, in the 1922 U.S. Open with his first national championship in 1923 by winning the U.S. Open at the age of 21.

That victory ignited an incredible run through the Roaring Twenties, during which Jones captured 13 major championships. During the same period, he finished second no less than four times in the U.S. Open and twice lost in the finals of the U.S. Amateur.

One of his second-place finishes in the Open came after Jones called a penalty on himself because his ball moved. No one else saw the ball move. When he was praised for his honesty, Jones seemed put off. "You might as well praise someone for not robbing a bank," he retorted.

He was born Robert Tyre Jones, Jr. His father was a lawyer who was nicknamed "The Colonel." Upon completing his studies, the younger Jones followed his father into practice.

To the world he was Bobby. To his friends he was Bob.

Jones seemed to epitomize everything American at the time. He was handsome enough to be a matinee idol. In fact, after his retirement from competition, Jones was persuaded to make a series of instructional golf films for Warner Brothers featuring the likes of W.C. Fields and other Hollywood celebrities in cameo roles. The films were shown as short subjects in movie theaters. They were rereleased on home video some 50 years later and outsold every other golf video released that year.

He was stylish, too. No one swung a golf club quite like Bobby Jones. He wasn't just good; he looked good. So damned good in fact, that when Jones was playing it was common for other competitors in adjacent fairways to stop and watch.

On top of it all, Jones was an extraordinarily bright man, as evidenced by his academic success. Unlike so many other athletes, he actually wrote his own autobiography without a ghostwriter, as well as his own instructional books and articles.

I was fast becoming an expert on this extraordinary man. And like most converts, I was enthusiastic about my newfound religion. Ken Cheatwood loaned me Jones's autobiography, *Down the Fairway*, and I finished it over a weekend. I then located copies of Jones's other books and magazine articles and read them as well.

It was evident that there was much to admire about Jones besides his golf exploits. He was clearly a remarkable man apart from his achievements as a player.

After withdrawing from competitive golf in 1930, the year he won the "Grand Slam," Jones went on to establish the Augusta National Golf Club, building the course on the grounds of an old fruit orchard. It was a spectacular achievement, coming during the Depression, and fulfilled Jones's dream of a special place where he and his friends could enjoy golf away from the intense public attention that seemed to follow him even in retirement. (Not long after he quit competitive golf, Jones arrived unannounced to play a friendly round at the Old Course at St. Andrews while "on holiday." Word spread throughout the town that Jones was on the course. By the time he reached the fifth hole, several thousand spectators had gathered to follow him.)

Not content just with having a place to play, Jones then decided to establish an invitational tournament so he could have an annual reunion with the great players of professional and amateur golf. He scheduled it to take place just as baseball's spring training ended in the Deep South, hoping to entice prominent national sportswriters to cover the event as they made their way by train back to the Northeast.

The inaugural event was held in 1934 and was called the Augusta National Invitational Tournament. Others in the club, most notably cofounder Cliff Roberts, wanted to call the tournament "The Masters." Although Jones felt that the title was too pretentious, he eventually relented, and the tournament soon was officially known by that name. Within 20 years, it was considered one of the major championships in professional golf along with the U.S. Open, the British Open, and the PGA Championship. Such was the magic of Bobby Jones.

Unfortunately, fate was as cruel to Jones in later life as it favored him in his youth. As The Masters grew, Jones's health began to trouble him. In the late 1940s, he was diagnosed with syringomyelia, a chronic progressive disease of the spinal cord with no known cause or cure. In a few years, Jones was forced to view The Masters from a golf cart. Not long thereafter, he was confined to a wheelchair. By all accounts, the disease attacked with astonishing force and humbled a body that at one time performed the most difficult athletic feats with a style and grace far beyond the reach of other men.

Even in Jones's final days, he would not let the disease steal his dignity. He never complained of his obvious pain and refused to discuss his condition with anyone other than his doctors. When the end came in 1971 at the age of 69, those who remained close to Jones were more impressed by the courage and grace that he displayed in the last painfilled years of his life than they were by his many golf achievements.

Unlike most sports figures, Jones continued to grow in stature after retiring from the arena of competition. And that truly set him apart.

Although he was "to the manor born," having advantages that few professionals of his era enjoyed, Jones was always well-liked by the professionals against whom he competed. While he didn't pretend to be one of them, he was never con-

descending toward them, either. He respected the professionals, and so he gained their respect as well. Far from
resenting the intrusion of this privileged amateur into their
midst, the touring pros relished the challenge he posed as one
artist might admire the work of another.

So it was that Jones became fast friends with Gene Sarazen,
Walter Hagen, Horton Smith, "Wild Bill" Mehlhorn, and
other contemporaries, as well as Sam Snead, Ben Hogan, and
Byron Nelson, who came along a decade later. And their affection for Jones made The Masters an important tournament
almost instantly.

As I read the accounts of Jones's tournament play, I recognized virtually all of the names of the prominent golfers of his
day. In addition to the professionals, there was Francis
Ouimet, Johnny Goodman, Jess Sweetser, and Charles Evans,
Jr., on the amateur side. They were all Jones's rivals and, for
the most part, his friends as well. Many of them were his
teammates on the Walker Cup, a competition between teams
of amateurs from the United States and Great Britain/Ireland
held every other year. Jones played on five straight teams and
was the playing captain for the last two competitions in which
he participated, in 1928 and 1930.

In the middle of all this, I came across an account of Jones's
play in the 1928 Southern Amateur, held at the famed Seminole
Golf Club in Florida. The story described how, at each stage of
match play, Jones defeated the leading amateurs. The one
name I didn't recognize was his semifinal opponent: Beauregard
Stedman. Stedman must have been some player; he eliminated

Jones from the competition in a match that lasted 20 holes before Stedman won by making a 40-footer for birdie.

I had never heard of this Stedman fellow. There was a small picture of him, but the paper was so faded his features were blurred. He appeared to be fairly short, no more than 5′ 6″ or so. But he was thick in the chest and his uprolled sleeves (they still played in long-sleeved shirts and ties) showed the kind of forearms that appeared strong enough to strangle an opponent if he had a mind to. His build made me think of Ian Woosnam. The big difference was that Stedman appeared to have a wild head of hair, sandy in color and tightly curled. From the looks of the picture, it hadn't seen a comb in a while, either.

His game must have been as spectacular as his appearance. The account of the match insisted that Stedman routinely outdrove Jones — who was considered very long off the tee — by as much as 30 yards. Only Jones's magic with Calamity Jane, his putter, extended the match 20 holes before he was eliminated.

The article described Stedman as a young phenom, only 15 years old. For someone that young to beat Jones was remarkable. At the time, Jones already had eight major championship trophies on his mantle and was the best known golfer in the world. Yet Stedman had matched Jones par for par and birdie for birdie until he was able to win at the 20th hole. As an indication of the quality of their play, both players shot 68 for the first 18 holes of their match.

For young Stedman, it must have been the thrill of a lifetime to beat the greatest player in the world. Not surprisingly, the final was reported to be something of an anticlimax after Jones was eliminated from the field. Perhaps exhausted by his monumental victory over Jones, Stedman lost 2 and 1 to Jess Sweetser.

I had never seen Beau Stedman's name mentioned before in any of my reading. Jones was quite generous in his autobiography with his fellow players, calling many of them by name and always complimenting their games. His book recounted numerous war stories of the great matches he had played. Yet I didn't recall any mention of his match with Stedman in the Southern Amateur.

Of course, Jones competed against a lot of people, and it simply wasn't possible for him to name all of them. Still, I found myself wondering what became of Beau Stedman. In fact, I became more interested in that than in my indexing of Jones's other papers. Not that anyone cared; no one had asked to see the results of my labors even after three weeks on the job.

I guess I should have been jealous. Most of the other law clerks were working directly with lawyers in the firm on various research projects. A couple of them had been allowed the privilege of attending depositions to observe how real lawyers work. One lucky clerk even got to watch a senior partner argue a motion in federal court.

For some reason, I really wasn't worried about whether the powers that be at the firm even knew whether Charley Hunter was alive. Ken Cheatwood and a couple of the other clerks had gotten interested in what I was doing, and they kept me in the loop of things, making sure I got invited along whenever the lawyers took the clerks out. I even made a Braves game, watching Tom Glavine beat the Mets 4-2.

I don't even remember wondering why I wasn't jealous. I suppose I was having too much fun back in the 1920s.

Chapter 3

WHEN I WAS A CHILD, I came across a couple of old scrapbooks that belonged to my mother. They became my favorite reading material for years. I would spend hours looking over the old photographs of my grandparents, my mother and uncles, and their friends.

The stuff from the 1940s, when my grandparents were young, was my favorite. The '40s seemed like such a romantic time to me, what with World War II and all. My grandparents had saved programs and dance cards from formals and other social events. There were even mementos from mixers in college. My grandmother had even saved newspaper clippings about the war, particularly those that mentioned boys with whom she had gone to school.

My infatuation with that era continued to adulthood. I preferred watching black and white films made in the '40s, in which the men wore suits and the women wore gowns, than most any current Hollywood production. It was no coincidence to me that more and more of Hollywood's output now consisted of remakes of the old classics.

I now had another set of scrapbooks, so to speak, and I was reading them with the same fascination as my mother's memorabilia. It reminded me of the wonderful journeys I had made back in time as a youngster and was certainly more fun than any other project I could have been given.

Part of it was the elegance of the time. In the magical decade before the Depression when Jones dominated golf, the great championships of his sport were held at upper crust country clubs far removed from anything the average man or woman would ever see. It was the time of Great Gatsby. Golfers played in ties, and, in the true style of the rich, they did not sweat; they only perspired.

Golf's amateurs were usually members of these posh clubs and enjoyed all their amenities. However, although professionals were occasionally allowed to play their courses, they usually dressed in their cars because entry into the clubhouse was forbidden to them.

With few exceptions, amateur golfers were rich men who had gone to college and then into banking, law, or business. Professional golfers, on the other hand, had little education and came to the game as caddies. They played the game for money because they had no other way to make a decent living.

Class lines were fairly clear in those days, and sportswriters usually fell on the side of the line with the professionals as opposed to the amateurs. America was not an egalitarian place then, and class differences were keenly felt. This may have accounted for the fact that the professional side of the game received excellent coverage from the sportswriting fraternity, which probably felt it was championing its own. When it came right down to it, the only real difference in their eyes between Babe Ruth and Walter Hagen was that they played different sports.

The real breakthrough, however, came at the 1931 U.S. Open at Inverness in Toledo, when the club invited the professionals into the clubhouse and allowed them the use of the locker room. For the touring pros, this was a major social advance. They were so grateful that they later presented the club with a grandfather clock inscribed in appreciation, which remains on display there to this day.

These historical events were coming alive in the aging and frayed files that lay in my hands. I was reading accounts of tournaments Jones played on the great courses of Long Island, New York, such as Garden City, Maidstone, and Shinnecock Hills. If any place epitomized the world of Gatsby, it was the Hamptons.

Then, in the midst of my reverie over what it must have been like, a name leapt off the page at me: Beauregard Stedman. He had beaten George Von Elm 5 and 4 in the finals of the 1929 Garden City Invitational.

I hurried down the hall to Cheatwood's office.

"Look at this."

Cheatwood immediately put down the deposition he was

summarizing and read what I handed him.

"Do you know anything about this guy Von Elm?"

"Yeah. I recognize the name. He was good." He reached over to a stack of books he kept in his office. Pulling down one I was becoming familiar with, he began to read.

"According to this, Von Elm was no pushover. He and Jones squared off in the finals of the U.S. Amateur twice, each coming away with the title once."

"You mean this guy was a U.S. Amateur champ?"

"That's what it says here." He pointed to the page. "And I'll tell you something else: Garden City is a great golf course. Back in college, I got invited to play there. It was right after I made All-American my junior year. Great track."

He pulled down another book. "Let's see . . . yeah, I was right. Garden City's been the site of several U.S. Amateurs. I know it's still listed in virtually every ranking of great courses in the United States."

The article I had shown Cheatwood described the same kind of powerful play that Stedman had displayed against Jones in the Southern Amateur at Seminole a year earlier. In a 36-hole final, Stedman had apparently taken charge early, jumping out to a 3-up lead after 18 holes, and had closed Von Elm out with 4 holes left in the 36-hole final. There was even a picture showing Stedman, with his distinguished woolly hair all askew, grinning and holding the winner's cup aloft.

As he handed it back to me, Cheatwood asked, "How did Jones make out in the tournament?"

"You know, there's no mention of him."

My friend gave me a puzzled look. "That's odd. Even playing below his usual standards, I would have expected him to do well enough in the medal rounds to qualify for match play. He was such a great player. If he had failed to advance to the match play bracket, that would have been news in itself. There's no mention of him at all?"

I held out the article. "See for yourself."

He shook his head. "No, I believe you. It's just strange. It sounds like Jones didn't enter the tournament." Cheatwood paused thoughtfully. "But if that's the case, what's this clipping doing in his files?"

I had no answer, so I went back to my cell. It wasn't long before another clipping caught my eye. This one recited the results of the 1929 Metropolitan Open, which had been held on the East Course at Winged Foot in Mamaroneck, New York, just three months later. It was a 72-hole stroke play event, and I immediately noticed the name of Beau Stedman, who must have been all of 16 years of age at the time, finishing third at 284 behind Walter Hagen with 281 and Ralph Guldahl with 283.

In a span of 90 days in early 1929, Beau Stedman had finished first and third in two of the most prestigious golf tournaments in the country. And he was barely old enough to shave. I wanted to share this with Cheatwood, but he had been called into the office of one of the lawyers to discuss the status of a project he was working on. I went back to work.

The next sheet of paper in the file was a crudely written note of some kind. It read: *Thoght you might like to see thez. I played pretty good. Thanks to you.* It was unsigned. Although it had no address or salutation, it had apparently been sent to Jones.

Now what on earth was this, I wondered. Then it hit me. This note had enclosed the clippings about Beau Stedman. Could it have been written by Stedman himself? If so, why was he sending a note of gratitude to Jones? What had Jones done for Stedman? There was obviously some connection, but I had no clue what it was.

At the time, Stedman was around 16 years of age, and Jones was 27. Judging from Stedman's poor spelling, he had little education and was certainly not of Jones's social class. Thus, they would hardly have been friends outside of golf, and they didn't seem to be related in any way either. The dark side of me momentarily speculated that perhaps Stedman was a half-brother, the result of some indiscretion by the Colonel.

Or maybe it was something far less titillating. Maybe Jones had simply taken an interest in an outstanding young player who had the potential to be his equal in golf.

There were any number of explanations for the note, and I had no evidence leading me to believe one was more likely than the others. One thing I did notice was that Stedman was still listed as an amateur in the Metropolitan Open standings. He had accepted no prize money. He remained eligible to pursue the grand prizes of amateur golf, such as the U.S. Amateur and the British Amateur, as well as such notable tournaments as the Western, Northeast, and Southern amateur championships. But traveling the amateur circuit cost money, and there was nothing to indicate that Stedman had the means to do so.

As I sat there with these faded remnants of the past laying before me, I could not resist indulging in more speculation. Why hadn't Stedman turned pro? The third-place prize money from the Metropolitan had to be tempting. If indeed he wrote the note to Jones, Stedman was not educated to the degree one would expect for an amateur golfer of his day. Thus, I concluded (without any real justification) that Jones somehow had become Stedman's patron.

If so, the arrangement did not last long.

Several pages deeper into the file, I came across a chilling news clipping. The headline read: "Manager's Wife Murdered at Hilton Head Club." Beneath it in smaller print: "Transient Golf Pro Prime Suspect." That "prime suspect" was none other than Beauregard Stedman. The article, dated January 27, 1930, described how Harold Gladstone, the manager of Crimson Bank's Golf Club, had found his wife's bloodstained body in their residence at the club. The clipping described in graphic detail how she had been stabbed 47 times, although it didn't say who had the unhappy duty of counting the wounds. The distraught husband accused Stedman, who was said to have worked at the club as an assistant pro, of the murder.

From what I gathered, the title "assistant pro" in those days was a euphemism that really meant someone who was a combination caddy master, janitor, club repairer, locker room attendant, and golf course superintendent. At least that's what one of the books I filched from Cheatwood's portable library indicated.

The "assistant pro" was just that — an assistant to the pro. He was generally taken from the ranks of the caddies, and no additional training was required for the job. It was a better job than others at the club only because there were more opportunities for tips and some of the work was indoors.

In the winter months, an assistant pro repaired equipment, cleaned gutters, and did whatever else needed to be done to get the club and course ready for the next season. Stedman apparently had signed on to earn some travel money during the winter break for the following year. Those in charge of administering the rules of amateur status probably would have overlooked Stedman's title given the nature of his duties, but it was nonetheless ironic that, in addition to being accused of murder, Stedman was coincidentally described as being a professional — less than a year after declining to accept prize money from the Metropolitan Open.

Aside from confirming that Stedman was not of the privileged class, the report showed that, if Jones had indeed become Stedman's sponsor, he had made a big mistake. Stedman was apparently a killer.

Chapter 4

I REALLY DIDN'T EXPECT to find anything more about Beau Stedman among Jones's papers. The sobering headline about Mrs. Gladstone's murder had put a quick end to my speculation. So much for theories about connections between Jones and Stedman. Jones would never have gotten close to someone capable of murder.

No, I decided, there was nothing more to this than Jones encouraging a talented young player, who in turn was predictably impressed by the attentions of the world's greatest player. Stedman's note with a couple of news clippings was simply an attempt to maintain the connection. Obviously, I reasoned, this casual relationship, which was limited to the golf course, ended when Stedman was exposed as a murderer.

All of this served to remind me that reconstructing history from limited information was tricky business.

Cheatwood agreed. "Charley, you're like those guys who find a few dinosaur bones and try to figure out what the whole animal looked like. You have to be real careful. I guess that's why they recently killed off the brontosaurus, which was my favorite dinosaur as a kid."

He laughed at his own reminiscence. "Everybody else always chose Tyrannosaurus Rex. I suppose I had to be different by choosing a gangly, slow-moving plant-eater."

I still didn't catch on to what he was saying. "What do you mean they killed it off?"

"Turns out it was just a theory based on insufficient evidence; they had put the skull of one dinosaur on the body of another."

"So Stedman was my brontosaurus, huh?"

"Looks that way."

I comforted myself with the hope that one door closing meant another one would soon open. So I went back to reading Jones's papers to see what other stories they might disclose. Even without Stedman, any details about Jones's life made for good reading.

It wasn't long before I came across another clipping. This one was apparently a sequel to the original story about Mrs. Gladstone's murder. According to this article, Stedman had disappeared at the time of the murder. No one knew where he was. The police were quoted as saying that they had no leads concerning his whereabouts.

Right behind that clipping was another note that had been sent to Jones. It was written in the same hand as the earlier one.

You know I wooden do nothin so bad, the note read. *But what chance have I got? They say I will get the chare. I don't want to die for sumthin I did not do.*

Then I saw other notes in a more familiar handwriting that matched the writing in other files. In his distinctive hand, Jones had scribbled, GR 653. 9:00.

What was this, I wondered. The first number could have been anything, from a license plate number to a county road designation. The second number most likely indicated the time of nine o'clock. Was this a note to meet someone at a particular place and time?

It occurred to me that the note may not have anything to do with the other file contents. It was just a scrap of paper. Perhaps it found its way into the file by accident.

Then it dawned on me that the most likely meaning of the cryptic abbreviation written in Jones's hand was a telephone number and, apparently, a time to call it. Back then, numbers reached only five digits, with the first two representing the initial letters of the exchange.

But that meant that Jones may have been talking with an escaped murderer. What on earth, I wondered, would motivate him to do such a thing?

I read on. There was another note, again in Jones's hand, that simply said, *Harrisburg. Merkel Farms. Ask for Ben Davis.* If this was related to Stedman at all, perhaps it was a witness who could help him. Or a new employer. It could even be an alias. There was no way of knowing.

I came across still another note. It had the same hand-writing and fractured spelling as the previous ones I had attributed to Stedman. It was also just as cryptic:

Played the Northeast Amateur. Shot 68, 75 (got nervus). Used Ben Davis. After maches started, a man asked questuns. So I left.

So that was it. Stedman was still trying to play by using an alias. Perhaps it was borrowed from a real person by that name in Harrisburg.

At lunch that day, I told Cheatwood that I was back to dinosaur hunting and shared my new findings with him.

"It seems kind of stupid to me," I told my fellow clerk-cum-golf reference. "How could he expect to get away with that?"

Cheatwood laughed. "Until a few years ago, you could walk through airport security and board any airplane you wanted without anyone even checking your ticket. You could buy an airline ticket in any name you wanted. No one checked to see if you were the person whose name was on the ticket. You think amateur golf tournaments 50 years ago had better security than airports?"

"So it really wasn't a dumb idea," I conceded.

"Unless someone knew him, he could pull it off. I don't know why he stayed in the East, though. I'd have lit out for other parts of the country. Maybe California. Plenty of golf tournaments there."

I laughed. "Doesn't sound like you trust the criminal justice system, either."

"You know what kind of lawyer a poor schmuck like Stedman would get? Some public defender. Overworked and underpaid. No thanks. Back then, you didn't need a witness protection program in order to disappear and start a new life."

I had to admit that Cheatwood made sense. This was before Social Security, television, or the Internet. There was no Big Brother. As I returned from lunch to the cell we now called the "Jones Room," I pondered these questions without finding an answer. I could only hope that the answers were ahead of me in one of the unopened files.

Then it hit me. Jones was a lawyer. Why couldn't he represent Stedman? While criminal law wasn't his specialty, a lawyer of Jones's caliber with no experience in criminal law was better than some beleaguered and barely competent sap experienced only in failure. Besides, the effect of having one of the most recognizable sports figures in the world walk into a courtroom as your lawyer had to be electrifying.

Indulging in that fantasy only prompted more questions. Criminal lawyers are inevitably sullied by their clients. Why would Jones want to link himself in such a public way with a murderer? I felt foolish for even thinking that a man of his stature would risk such controversy. It would have been totally contrary to his image.

Then I saw a file with the label "People v. Stedman." Inside was a series of letters between Jones and Henry Montgomery, the District Attorney for Bankens County, South Carolina.

So Jones had become involved after all. Reading through the letters, his reasons for doing so became clear.

The first letter was dated February 3, 1930.

Dear Mr. Montgomery, Jones wrote. *I have learned of an unfortunate event occurring in your jurisdiction in which a young man named Beauregard Stedman is suspected of being involved in foul play leading to the death of a Mrs. Gladstone.*

I have known Mr. Stedman for many years, as he was a caddy at East Lake Country Club here in Atlanta where I played most of my golf. Though I do not have personal knowledge of the facts, I feel reasonably certain that Beau is incapable of murder. I understand that he cannot be located. He is no doubt frightened. If he happens to contact me, I will encourage him to meet with the authorities to clear this up. In the meantime, have you developed any evidence that would reveal the real culprit?

Montgomery's reply came a week later. *Dear Mr. Jones,* it began. *Thank you for your inquiry into the Gladstone murder. Mr. Stedman is indeed fortunate to have such a prominent reference as you. Will you be representing him?*

It was Montgomery's way of saying, okay, I'm impressed. But I've got a murder on my hands, and I want to find this guy. By asking Jones if he would be representing Stedman, Montgomery was trying to place him in a box. As an officer of the court, Jones might become obligated to surrender his client to the authorities.

Jones obviously understood the delicacy of his situation. In a letter dated February 20, 1930, he advised Montgomery that *I have not been retained on behalf of Mr. Stedman. I would imagine, however, that his reluctance to surrender to authorities might be overcome if he were persuaded that the investigation into the crime had proceeded beyond the bare accusation of the victim's husband, who did not witness the crime.*

Has Mr. Gladstone been eliminated as a suspect? If so, on what basis? Did he or the late Mrs. Gladstone have romantic interests outside their marriage? As you are no doubt aware, there are numerous questions that inevitably arise in a case like this, and I have seen nothing in the newspapers to answer these questions after Mr. Gladstone's well-publicized accusation of Mr. Stedman

Montgomery saw right through the polite language to the real message. What Jones really wanted to know was whether he was doing his job. A scared teenager with a poor background was a tempting — and easy — target. Instead of a laborious investigation with potentially endless rabbit trails, it would be much easier (as well as politically expedient) to coerce a bogus confession out of someone as hapless as Stedman.

Montgomery's next letter was more direct.

My friends in Atlanta tell me that you are as fine a lawyer as you are a golfer. They are unaware, however, of your ever handling a single criminal case. Perhaps that is the reason you asked questions that someone more experienced in these matters would consider impertinent.

I am not a champion golfer. I would never presume to give you advice on how to play the game. Kindly extend me the same courtesy.

That's where the paper trail ended. It left me rather unsatisfied. I wondered whether Jones knew where Stedman was. What kind of communication had taken place between them? Something had to have transpired. It just didn't seem likely that Jones would have taken it upon himself to intercede on Stedman's behalf.

At least I had learned about the origins of Jones's relationship with Stedman. East Lake was the place where Jones learned to play golf as a child. The pro there was a Scotsman named Stewart Maiden. He is generally credited with having taught the game to Jones, and he remained Jones's only real teacher throughout his life.

Back in the days before golf carts, virtually every golf course had caddies. This was especially true of country clubs. East Lake would have been no different.

I knew a little about East Lake. For many years it had been one of the finest clubs in Georgia. However, the neighborhood around it began to decline and, with it, so did the club's fortunes. In recent years, however, East Lake had been rejuvenated by a developer who spent millions on the club as well as the surrounding neighborhood. The clubhouse had been restored to its former grandeur, and its walls were covered with pictures of Jones.

The course had been magnificently restored as well, and major golfing events, including the PGA Tour's season-ending Tour Championship, soon returned to its fairways. East Lake became one of Atlanta's great success stories, one of those rare instances in which an urban renewal project had actually succeeded, no doubt in large part because it had been funded and managed by the private sector.

So Stedman had been a caddy at East Lake. That made sense. I imagined that Jones must have taken a liking to him and, when he showed a talent for the game, encouraged him along.

Still, Jones wouldn't have harbored a fugitive. That would have been unethical. Looking deeper in the file, I found scraps of paper with telephone numbers and names. Was this evidence of communication with Stedman? Were these other aliases? Or were they witnesses that Jones believed might clear Stedman's name?

That's when I found the letter.

Chapter 5

IT WAS A REMARKABLE document, a carbon copy of an undated letter written in Jones's own hand to his friend Beau Stedman. For reasons that soon became clear, Jones apparently preferred not to dictate the letter to a secretary for typing, and he wanted no address on the letter if it was discovered. However, he obviously did want some record of this communication with his troubled young friend.

My dear Beauregard, Jones wrote. *As a lawyer, I cannot encourage anyone to evade authorities who are investigating a crime. I had hoped, from my contact with the District Attorney in South Carolina, to obtain evidence that would persuade you to return there and help clear this matter up. However, I must admit that I was not pleased by his response. I am not your attorney; if I were, certain obligations might require me to dis-*

close your location. Even now, it would relieve me to know that, upon receiving this letter, you found a new place to stay. It is something of a burden for me to know where you are.

Jones was clearly wrestling with his professional obligations and felt a need to explain his thinking on paper.

He continued:

However, I am your friend as well as a lawyer. I cannot in good conscience tell you to surrender when I see no real interest among the authorities in finding who is really responsible for the terrible thing that was done. I know that you could not have done this, but it appears that it is more convenient to blame you than to discover the truth.

I know that you love the game as I do. As I told you many times, your talent for it is evident. Until this unfortunate mess, I expected to find your name on many of the same trophies that bear mine. It pains me to think that such a great thing does not appear possible under the present circumstances.

I cannot pretend to know the despair you must feel. I have never known a golfer who seemed so certain of his destiny. You have talked of nothing but championships since you were quite young. Now you cannot risk the exposure that pursuing championships will bring. I hope and pray that your passion for excellence can be redirected to other pursuits that give you some solace.

It was signed, *As ever, Bob.*

I put Jones's letter down and sat still for a long time. I tried to imagine how Beau Stedman must have felt when he read it. He was being cheated out of a place in golf history, and Jones was telling him to give it up.

It was, by any standard, a terrible injustice. I thought about what I would have done if I had been Stedman. My immediate reaction, I knew, would have been to reject Jones's advice. But then what? No alternatives came readily to mind.

Pursuing golf was out of the question with a murder charge pending. And the only way for Stedman to be cleared under the circumstances was to do it himself. Given the authorities' apparent desire for a scapegoat, that meant identifying the real killer with proof that could not be challenged.

However, it was apparent that someone in Stedman's circumstances simply wasn't able to discover and gather that kind of proof. Any effort on his part to investigate the crime would almost certainly attract attention, which would serve only to get him arrested. Once Stedman was behind bars, the focus of the entire system would be to convict him of the crime, and even token efforts to consider other suspects would end.

After conceding the futility of poor Stedman's situation, I finally returned to the papers in the file. When I did, I found his reply to Jones's discouraging letter.

Dear Mr. Jones,

Thank you for your letter. I have moved so don't worry. Your a good frend. I will win my champinships. Yes I will. Wate and see.

I'll rite agin.

Beau

There can be a fine line between courage and stupidity. At that moment, I couldn't tell which side of the line Stedman was on.

Chapter 6

WHILE MOST OF my time was absorbed by my detective work, I did enjoy an occasional diversion.

One afternoon several of us were invited to Peachtree Golf Club for lunch and a round of golf. I hadn't been playing much and looked forward to the game.

Peachtree was known as the other club started by Bobby Jones. It was founded in 1948, and Jones's involvement supposedly rankled some of Augusta's membership at the time. Not surprisingly, Peachtree enjoyed an outstanding reputation from the very beginning, not only because of its link to Jones but also because of the quality of its golf course. As evidence of the latter, the USGA chose Peachtree as the site of the 1989 Walker Cup competition.

Jones's memory was treated with the same reverence at Peachtree as it was at Augusta (and most everywhere else in

Georgia, for that matter). That wasn't always a good thing. For instance, when he started the club, Jones had suggested that membership be limited to 275. Over the years, despite a great demand, the club refused to budge from that number, for no other reason than it was the number chosen by Jones.

However, by the 1980s, the average age of Peachtree's membership had surpassed 70, and few of the members were active golfers any more. The Peachtree superintendent often lamented that he maintained a great course for no one to play. In fact, the course was so deserted at times that some members used the fairways as a practice range, hitting shag balls without ever interrupting play.

Even so, the members stubbornly refused to resign so that the numerous candidates on the club's rather sizeable waiting list could take their place. This was one of "Bobby's clubs," and, even if they only used it for an occasional lunch, the members weren't going anywhere, not even to transfer their membership to their own children.

However, even Jones's intimates were mortal. By the end of the 1980s the old membership was dying faster than a bad comedian, and the club took on a different look as new members quickly took to its fairways.

The contrast between the old and new membership was immediately apparent upon our arrival at the club. The new members were dressed in golf clothes; the old members wore business suits. The new members were animated; the old members were subdued. The new members were in their 40s or 50s; the old members were in their 70s or 80s. I suspected that the oldtimers resented the newcomers because, after all, they hadn't even known Bobby Jones.

Fred Nathan was hosting us for lunch and golf. He had invited Ken Cheatwood, me, and Barry Horn, a second-year clerk from Harvard Law School. Horn was an Atlanta native, but he had never been to Peachtree and was just as excited about it as Cheatwood and I were. He was also getting the big rush from the firm, which wanted him to work in its estate and tax section.

Fred Nathan had been a member at Peachtree for three years or so. Like the other "new members," Nathan had not personally known Jones. But being a lawyer with Jones's old law firm and having three senior partners who had known Jones — and had been members at Peachtree for many years— hadn't hurt.

Fred was obviously proud to be a part of Peachtree. He gave us a tour of the clubhouse on arrival and showed us the photos and other memorabilia of Jones on display. It was quite impressive.

There were photographs showing Jones and other founding members at the groundbreaking. There were photographs showing Jones playing the first round when the course opened. Some of his clubs were mounted for display, too, as well as balls he had used in competition.

The clubhouse was comfortably appointed. It seemed to match Jones's personality: dignified and unpretentious. And it smelled of old money. There was a library, or reading room, with a fireplace and leather wingback chairs. Two older members were quietly reading what I assumed was either the *Atlanta Constitution* or the *Wall Street Journal*. I wondered whether they were men of achievement or simply part of what Cheatwood called the "lucky sperm club."

In this environment, it didn't take long for me to start thinking about Jones's connection with Beau Stedman. Over lunch, Fred Nathan naturally asked each of us how our summer was going. He wanted to know how we liked the work.

When he came to me, I told him about discovering this great player in whom Jones had taken a fervent interest, to the point of shielding him from authorities who sought him for questioning in a murder case. He smiled politely, in the agreeable way of someone at a cocktail party, but clearly did not find the subject as interesting as I did.

"Charley, I bet you're going to find a lot of stories in those files. Bobby Jones was a very famous person. His celebrity attracted a lot of people. There's no telling what kinds of oddballs came out of the woodwork to approach him. Remember, next to Babe Ruth, Jones was probably the most recognized athlete of his day. I can imagine this kind of thing happened all the time to him."

"But I don't see any sign that Jones thought this guy was crazy or anything like that," I responded. "He had been a caddy at East Lake. Jones wrote a letter vouching for his character when he got in trouble."

Nathan smiled. "Jones was a gracious man. From everything I hear, he had trouble saying no to any well-intended request.

He would politely endure the most rude interruptions by strangers who approached him during meals or golf or whatever without ever becoming angry or upset. Maybe it was his Southern breeding. Maybe it was his character. Who knows. But it would have been like him to write something nice about some poor caddy who had gotten into trouble."

"This was more than that," I insisted. But I could tell I was getting nowhere, and we changed the subject.

I quickly forgot my disappointment when we teed off. Peachtree lived up to its reputation as a test of golf. Cheatwood was true to form, shooting 74. Horn and Nathan were not as good but played well enough. Both scored in the mid to high 80s.

I was pleasantly surprised by the quality of Nathan's game. His bookish appearance had led me to expect far less competence at the game than he demonstrated.

As for myself, I fit somewhere in the middle, shooting an 83 with the benefit of a mulligan. It seemed like every time I got something going I stopped myself with a double bogey.

In the 19th hole afterward, Nathan introduced me to an old member we encountered named Harland Carruthers.

"Charley, Mr. Carruthers knew Bobby Jones. In fact, he's one of the charter members of our club."

I looked at Mr. Carruthers with heightened interest. He seemed pleased to see that I was impressed by the reference to his connection with Jones. In an exchange that he had no doubt been through hundreds of time, I asked him to tell me about Jones. He indicated that his father had been one of the

Colonel's clients. Eventually, the son of the client met the son of the lawyer, and the two became friends.

Mr. Carruthers spoke in paragraphs that were no doubt memorized from repetition but did not sound rehearsed. He had been through this so often that I was sure he felt certain of my next questions.

I threw him a curve, though. In a tone of voice that surprised me by its intensity, I asked the old gentleman, "Did you know Beau Stedman?"

He was apparently disappointed to be asked a question he had not practiced answering. "I don't believe so," he answered in a soft voice after an awkward pause. The poor fellow seemed almost embarrassed by his answer, as if he had just been tested and failed.

That more or less ended the exchange. After Carruthers shuffled away, Nathan gave me a mild reproach. "For a second, I thought you were going to put poor old Mr. Carruthers under cross."

I looked to Cheatwood for a little support, but he said nothing, so I mumbled an apology that I hadn't meant to embarrass anyone and changed the subject.

It disappointed me that one of Jones's old friends apparently had never heard of Stedman. I was now more determined than ever to find out what became of the man Jones may have been grooming as our next great golf champion. If I failed, Beau Stedman would remain the greatest player who never lived.

Chapter 7

MY INVESTIGATION SEEMED to stall for a while. I came across a number of files that were uninteresting, which is to say they did not relate to my increasingly myopic search for information about Beau Stedman's eventual destiny. I found it hard to concentrate on cataloging these files. It was a distraction. I was much keener on playing detective than on being a librarian.

After two days of this, I felt a little panicky. What if there was nothing else? I picked up the pace at which I was working, as if rushing through the files would increase the chances of finding more news about Stedman.

I did find some interesting tidbits along the way. There was correspondence from Jones booking transatlantic passage to Great Britain for the Walker Cup when it was contested at the Old Course at St. Andrews in 1926. I looked it up; that was the trip when Jones stayed over to win the first of his three British

Open championships.

When I told Cheatwood about it, he described British Open courses as being "Scarborough Fair golf." I didn't understand what he meant until he joked about playing out of the parsley, sage, rosemary, and thyme.

Jones's father and his law partners must have been very supportive of his golf exploits, for they indulged his lengthy absences from the office for these transatlantic trips. The files contained memos from Jones to the rest of the firm explaining his schedule, and they were written in a way that indicated his complete confidence in their approval. The file also contained several reply memos from Jones's partners wishing him well and indicating their deep pride in his accomplishments. I was not surprised; no one could have accomplished what Jones did without the support of those around him.

Nonetheless, I was becoming increasingly discouraged. A couple of more files, and still no sign of Stedman. I did not give up all hope, however, because none of the papers appeared to have any logical order. In fact, everything had apparently been thrown into these boxes without any particular rhyme or reason. Whoever packed them must have been in a hurry.

Thus, I knew that the very next file might just be the one I was looking for.

And I was right. I opened a file and picked up the scent again. I was back into Depression-era golf once more.

This file also had a large number of clippings on top. They

described amateur tournaments across the country during the 1930s. Jones had retired from competition by then, so these were reports of tournaments in which he did not compete. I quickly scanned them for Stedman's name, but was disappointed not to find a single mention of him.

After the clippings were handwritten notes. The writing was familiar.

Dear Bob,

I am okay. I find work here and there. Nuthin speshul. I am even giving golf lesons.

I have been playing, to. I have to make up names. So far it has worked.

I put my new address on the invelop, I know you tole me not to. Please rite. I get lonesum sumtimes.

Beau.

Jones was compelled to respond.

My dear friend,

Thank you for your recent letter. It was good to hear from you.

I am pleased that you are playing. However, there is a risk that you will be discovered. Please be careful. I am hopeful that the day will come when we can finally clear the air. Until then, you cannot be too careful.

I was also very pleased to hear that you are giving golf lessons. You have a remarkable talent for the game and can pass a lot of it along to others through teaching.

The game has many layers of meaning. I for one have never exhausted them. You will learn much about yourself from teaching others and peeling back as many layers as you can.

I think of you often. You are not alone.

As ever, Bob

Again, Jones had retained a copy of his handwritten letter. Since there was no longer any question about whether he was serving as Stedman's attorney, I wondered why he did so. He obviously wanted to retain a record of his correspondence to Stedman, but what for?

Perhaps he wanted evidence of the kind of suffering Stedman was being forced to endure, I mused. Perhaps he wanted the world to know one day the true extent of the injustice of this false accusation.

As a player, Jones had long understood the competitive necessity of accepting bad bounces. He once described how golf, more than any other game, could sear the soul with its dramatic changes of fortune. It was critical, he knew, not to be defeated by such adversity but to accept it with equanimity. Only then could it be overcome.

But he was apparently having some difficulty accepting Beau Stedman's bad bounce. And so I found a cache of letters between Stedman and Jones that revealed two men of vastly different backgrounds with much in common. They shared indomitable wills and a refusal to accept defeat. They both loved golf and had a great talent for it. And they both found in that game the means by which to survive the great trials of their lives. Stedman's test was first, coming tragically early in his life. Jones's was later, when he was struck by a crippling spinal disease.

I went back to the clippings.

Chapter 8

MALONE WINS STATE AM WITH RECORD SCORE

(Associated Press) Ocean Springs, Mississippi — Young Dave Malone, a carpenter from Natchez, nearly lapped the field here in winning the 1931 Mississippi State Amateur, posting a record score of 276 after 72 holes of play at the Gulf Hills Dude Ranch and Country Club. Malone posted 14 birdies and only two bogies in four rounds over the 6,650-yard layout known for its tight fairways and smallish greens.

"He just overpowered the course," said an admiring runner-up Phillip Martin, who finished ten strokes behind Malone. "He hit almost every par five in two, and he even drove the green on that short par four (the 310-yard 12th hole)."

Todd Andrews, from Jackson, quipped, "He said he just moved here. I don't know where he came from, but I wish he would go back and take his golf game with him." Andrews, the

1928 champion, finished fifth at 291, a whopping 15 strokes behind Malone.

Malone left quickly upon the conclusion of play and was unavailable for comment. The top results of the championship:

Dave Malone, Natchez	276
Phillip Martin, Jackson	286
Fred Graham, Greenville	289
Mike Passey, Brookhaven	289
Todd Andrews, Biloxi	291
Ray Carter, Jackson	292
John Peters, Jackson	292
Sam Bass, Starkville	293
George Miller, Bay St. Louis	295
Doug Anderson, Biloxi	295
Pete Warren, Ocean Springs	295
Hillary Johnson, Natchez	296
Terry Baylor, Oxford	297
Virgil Lee, Jackson	300
Tim Patterson, Hattiesburg	301
Olen Frazier, Jackson	301
Cleveland Wall, Brookhaven	302
Martin Castle, Tupelo	303
Robert Links, Moss Point	304
Craig Darrow, Jackson	305
Robert Timmons, Oxford	306
Scott Fussell, Picayune	306
Russell Landry, Brookhaven	307

Charles Withers, Biloxi	308
Paul McCall, Starkville	309
Eugene Meyers, Greenville	309
Carson Haley, Ocean Springs	310

So Beau Stedman had become Dave Malone. And he was still chasing championships. While a state amateur title was a notch or two below regionals like the Southern Amateur and the Northeast Amateur — and of course even farther removed from the U.S. Amateur — it was still good competition. Winning any golf tournament by such a large margin was an impressive performance.

Besides, it was no doubt easier to escape detection in smaller events. While the Mississippi story had been placed on the AP wire, I doubted that it had been picked up by any newspaper outside the state, with the possible exception of the New Orleans Picayune.

The next clipping showed that Beau was on the move.

AMATEUR TITLE TO WALKER

Special to *The Picayune* — Clarence Walker, a young construction worker from Destrehan, is the 1931 Louisiana State Amateur champion. He won the tournament in fine fashion, taking charge with a 68 in the first round to put him ahead of the field by two strokes and then increasing his lead with scores of 71, 69, and a final 67. The five-under score in the last round tied the competitive course record at the New Orleans Country Club, and Walker's total of 275 set a new tournament record. He outdistanced runner-up Jimmy McGonnagill of Monroe by eight shots.

Interviewed as he was leaving the course, a bashful Walker said, "I had a good week. The breaks went my way. The other fellows were good to play with."

Second-place finisher McGonnagill, a three-time champion, was impressed by Walker's play. "He's a lot longer than anybody out here. I never played with him before. He doesn't say much. He just goes about his business. I just couldn't keep up with him."

Defending champion Mark Quarles of Lafayette finished third. The top ten scores were:

Clarence Walker	275
Jimmy McGonnagill	283
Mark Quarles	285
Harold Simon	286
Cam Theriot	286
Gerald Collins	287
John Fontenot	288
Joe Guillory	288
Eddie Simien	289
Allen Trosclair	291

Beau had won another championship, and he made it look just as easy as the last one. He apparently hadn't moved very far to do it, either. I looked on a map and found Destrehan. It was a small town 30 miles or so from New Orleans.

I had to wonder where he was headed next. If Beau continued in the same direction, his next stop would be Texas. Then, again, maybe he would take Cheatwood's advice and go to California.

I also wondered if he knew the difference between going underground and digging his own grave.

Chapter 9

IF BEAU CONTINUED west and landed in Texas, he was going to find a much different world there. Most Texans considered themselves to be a republic rather than another state. If forced to do so, they would eventually concede to being an equal part of the United States. They just thought themselves to be a whole lot more equal than anyone else.

When it comes to golf, Texans probably have a right to feel that way. Texas golf can legitimately claim to be bigger and better than most anywhere else. Ever the golf history buff, Cheatwood explained to me that Texas had produced legendary players like Ben Hogan, Byron Nelson, Jimmy Demaret, Jackie Burke, Lee Trevino, and Dave Marr, to name but a few, as well as grand old courses like River Oaks in Houston, Preston Trail in Dallas, and Colonial in Fort Worth. As my buddy put it, "Texas can play with anyone."

Even though Texas summers are brutally hot during the time of year when the major championships are being played, the golf establishment has never hesitated to bring its majors to the Lone Star State. Thus, I was surprised to learn, Cedar Crest in Dallas hosted the PGA Championship way back in 1927, when Walter Hagen won the last of his five PGA titles. Dallas Athletic Club was the next Texas host of the PGA in 1963 (where the trophy became so hot sitting out in the sun that winner Jack Nicklaus had to hold it with a towel), followed by Pecan Valley in San Antonio in 1968. Colonial brought the U.S. Open to Fort Worth in 1941, Northwood in Dallas followed in 1952, and Champions Golf Club in Houston hosted the national championship in 1969. Champions has also hosted the Ryder Cup, the U.S. Amateur, the season-ending Tour Championship for the top 30 money winners of the PGA Tour, as well as countless other championships. As recently as 1991, Colonial hosted the U.S. Women's Open. Houston Country Club was the site of a classic match between Sam Snead and Ben Hogan on Shell's Wonderful World of Golf. The PGA Tour still makes annual visits to Houston, Dallas, Fort Worth, and San Antonio for regular Tour events.

Texas remains well-represented on the current pro tour, with several Texans being recent winners of major championships. Ben Crenshaw, who has won The Masters twice, hails from Austin. So does Tom Kite, who won the U.S. Open at Pebble Beach in 1992. In addition, former PGA champion Mark Brooks and recent British Open champion Justin

Leonard both call Dallas home.

I had known some of this already, but Ken Cheatwood filled me in on the rest. He was now checking on me a couple of times a day for updates on my investigation.

Ken and I had become fast friends. In less than a month, he had turned me into an avid student of golf tradition. Cheatwood really knew his stuff; he was the kind of guy who might eventually become a member of the USGA Executive Committee or at Augusta National. He truly loved all things golf, and his enthusiasm for the game and everything about it was infectious.

One afternoon I showed him the articles about Stedman winning the Mississippi and Louisiana tournaments. As he looked at the scores, he whistled.

"This guy was on a mission," he said. "He was really out to prove something."

He looked up. "You know, for some of these guys, winning golf tournaments was the only way they could have a better life. Look at Byron Nelson. He wanted a ranch. Every tournament he won brought him that much closer to it. He had that incredible run in 1945, winning — what was it? — 11 tournaments in a row. Jones must have loved this; of all things, it was an amateur who finally beat him in Memphis. Guy from New Orleans by the name of Freddie Haas. Nelson won 18 tournaments that year. By the end of the year, he had nearly enough money to buy his ranch and the cattle to go with it. Two years later, he was done. Quit at the age of 35. Never really played seriously after that. Can you believe it?"

He was watching me to make certain I understood the importance of what he was saying. "Hell, Ben Hogan didn't win most of his majors until after he turned 40. Imagine what Nelson might have done if he had stayed motivated."

I looked at Cheatwood. "You mean Nelson quit because he got his ranch?"

"That's right," Cheatwood nodded. "Said he had accomplished what he set out to do. His dream put the fire in his belly. Once it became reality, the fire went out."

He tapped on the paper in front of him. "There was a fire burning in Stedman. He had dreams of winning championships, and this was the only way he could do it, by going to smaller tournaments. Why else would he risk getting sent back to South Carolina to get fried for something he didn't do?"

I handed another sheet of paper to Cheatwood. "Then you'd better take a look at this."

He read a few minutes and then burst out laughing. "Ernest Hemingway? You've got to be kidding."

I couldn't resist a chuckle myself. "According to some of the other letters, he heard the name somewhere and liked the way it sounded. He didn't know it belonged to a famous author."

Cheatwood shook his head. "So he tried to use it as an alias to play in the Texas State Amateur?"

"That's right," I said. "He registered for the tournament using that name. When he got to the Texarkana Country Club, officials with the Texas State Golf Association were waiting for him. They must have thought he was a pro trying to sneak into the tournament. Anyway, they pulled him into a back room in the pro shop and started asking questions. Poor bastard must've been scared to death."

I held up another file. "According to this, he took off in his car and was in such a hurry that he was stopped by a deputy sheriff a few miles outside of town for speeding. When he couldn't produce a driver's license for his bail, they hauled him off to jail."

My buddy rolled his eyes in disbelief as I explained, "I don't know how he talked them into it, but somehow he got the jailer to let him make a phone call to Mr. Jones. Jones then wired the money to pay Stedman's fine, and he was sprung."

Cheatwood chuckled. "I bet he was glad to be out of there."

My friend sat there stroking his chin and thinking about what it must have been like. Shifting in his chair, he said, "Stedman was damned lucky. Texas was always light years ahead of most places when it came to golf. They were used to all kinds of hustlers and sandbaggers. Golf was a big money game in Texas back then. The people running their state tournaments were gonna pay a lot more attention to who entered than those folks in Mississippi and Louisiana."

He looked up. "Did he play in any more tournaments after that?"

I shook my head. "I don't know. But I would be surprised if he did. From what I can see in his letters to Mr. Jones, he must have been frightened out of his wits by the experience."

Cheatwood looked at his watch and jumped up. "Man, it's later than I thought. I've got to have a memo on fraudulent joinder on Mr. Benefield's desk in the morning." As he reached the door, he turned back and said cheerfully, "While I'm back to the grind, you keep reading, and let me know what you find."

After my fellow clerk left, I reentered the time warp in Jones's old files. I did not find any further attempts by Stedman to play in amateur tournaments. As I soon learned, he had turned his attention to much bigger game.

Chapter 10

IT WAS WELL KNOWN that Bob Jones was unshakeably loyal to his friends. When he placed New York financier Cliff Roberts in charge of Augusta National, the autocratic Roberts made numerous enemies with his brusque and unpredictable ways. For instance, a member once complained about a bunker. Roberts had it rebuilt and sent him the bill. That was Roberts's way of discouraging what he considered to be meddling in his domain. He was also known to warn members who complained about the way the club was run that it jeopardized their status with the club.

Roberts was judge, jury, and executioner when it came to club matters, and he punished those who violated its rules almost according to his whim. What made things worse was that many of the rules that Roberts enforced in such an intemperate style appeared to exist only in his head and could change on a day-to-day basis without notice. Through repeated controversies, however, Jones never wavered in his support of his friend.

For whatever reason, Jones had also developed the same kind of loyalty to Beau Stedman. Just as he forgave Roberts his sins, he also absolved Stedman of his. I imagined that both Roberts and Stedman must have taxed Jones's patience on occasion. Like Roberts, Stedman had a growing list of transgressions, to which the fiasco in Texas was the latest addition. But as I read the increasingly frequent correspondence between Jones and Stedman, it was clear that the bond between the two remained strong.

For one thing, Jones had to admire Stedman's perseverance. Despite great adversity, Stedman continued to support himself with hard work. Most of it was quite physical in nature, ranging from carpentry to heavy construction. Two things that Jones admired were hard work and great golf. Stedman had a talent for both.

It was also clear after the close call at Texarkana that Stedman couldn't compete on the regular amateur circuit any longer. Word about the incident no doubt spread quickly throughout the leading amateur golf associations around the country. Stedman would be a marked man from then on.

For this reason, the two comrades-in-arms had apparently been discussing an alternative plan to keep Stedman in competition. One of Jones's letters (he was still keeping copies in his files) explained the plan:

My dear Beau,

I agree that it would be imprudent for you to enter any more tournaments. The ones that are prominent enough to offer you good competition will also present the highest risk of discovery. The others aren't worth entering for a player of your abilities.

I also understand your intense need to compete. You have been blessed with remarkable talent, and it should be tested.

There is another way to go. Matches can be arranged between talented players outside of formal competition. In fact, with the right backing, you can play the world's finest players. I am fortunate enough to know virtually all of them, as well as people of means who would just as soon bet on a golf match as on a horse race. The idea of backing a player with great hidden talent like you against a well-known player will appeal to many of them.

Allow me time to make some arrangements. In the meantime, keep your game sharp.

As ever, Bob

Since I had embarked on this project, I had found many surprises along the way. However, nothing surprised me more than discovering Jones acting as a broker to arrange matches between Stedman and the greats of golf. This was a private side of Jones that had never been revealed to the public. Under the circumstances, though, it made perfect sense.

Most successful tournament players thrive on competition. According to Ken Cheatwood, the competition is a kind of addiction. Few of them care much for casual golf. If they're not competing in a tournament, then they're playing for high stakes in some betting game. As Cheatwood explained it to me, it has always been a common practice on the pro tour to engage in heavy betting during practice rounds. Many pros believe that it keeps them from developing careless habits that might carry over into formal competition.

Jones and the players of his day were no exception. For many of them, a three-foot putt wasn't worth laboring over unless something was riding on it.

For this reason, it didn't surprise me to find a letter from Jones to friends at the Boca Raton Club in Florida confirming arrangements for Stedman (under an assumed name) to play Tommy Armour in March of 1932. Although Armour was one of the best players in the world, he still needed the additional income of a winter job, and the Boca Raton Club was one of the finest resorts in the world. Just as Sam Snead did at Greenbriar, Armour supplemented his income nicely by giving "playing lessons," which meant that he charged the resort's well-heeled guests for the privilege of playing a few holes with him.

If Stedman was going to step up in class, it was going to be a big step. Tommy Armour was at the top of his game. Originally from Scotland, Armour lost an eye while fighting in World War I, yet went on to win the 1927 U.S. Open at Oakmont (beating Harry Cooper in a playoff), the 1930 PGA (defeating Gene Sarazen in the finals), and the 1931 British Open at Carnoustie. He nearly won the PGA again in 1935, losing to Johnny Revolta in the finals.

After facing death in the trenches in Europe, there was little about golf that could make Armour nervous. If Stedman was looking for another way to test his game, he could not possibly have found stiffer competition than the man whose nickname, the Silver Scot, was inspired by the color of his hair.

Each side agreed to put up $500, winner take all. The match would consist of 18 holes at stroke play, and whoever had the lower total after 18 holes would be declared the winner.

Stedman's backers were to pay his expenses and give him $100 if he won. It seemed to me that, after paying Stedman, they didn't stand to gain all that much from winning their bet, but these sports no doubt loved the idea of backing some unknown who might knock off the Silver Scot in his adopted backyard. Besides, they had to figure that any player recommended by Bob Jones was worth watching.

I can imagine their reaction, though, upon seeing Stedman for the first time, with his wild, woolly hair and all. The fact that he was all of 20 years old had to worry them, too. But they must have gotten over the shock eventually, because the match came off.

There couldn't have been a greater contrast between the contestants. Compared to the rough-around-the-edges Stedman, Armour was second only to Walter Hagen in deportment. He was a keen observer of the wealthy clientele at the resort, and, when he wasn't playing, he could be seen giving lessons on the practice tee while sitting in a chair drinking gin and tonic. Armour definitely had style.

Despite appearances, Armour took his teaching seriously. He was recognized by most of his contemporaries as a keen student of the game. In fact, he eventually wrote one of the best instructional books on golf ever published, *How To Play Your Best Golf All the Time.* (Naturally, my buddy Cheatwood had a copy.)

Although he was every bit as much a hustler as the other pros of his day, the dapper Scotsman probably didn't welcome this particular wager. It is no fun being challenged on your home turf, where there is always a potential for embarrassment, particularly when your opponent is a relative unknown. However, it would have been considered bad form to turn down the challenge.

Jones's file had copious notes and a letter from one of his friends in Boca Raton. Together, they provided a running commentary of sorts about the progress of the match. Someone had given Jones a remarkably detailed account of what transpired.

I thought it was unusual and said so to Cheatwood. He reminded me that golfers were notorious for recounting even the most ordinary round stroke by stroke. In fact, he told me that one of the oldest pro shop tricks in the book to cut short a member's boring replay of an entire round was to ask what club the narrator hit for his approach at the seventeenth hole. He said it was guaranteed to mercifully shorten the account by sixteen holes almost every time.

This was different, of course. This was no Thursday afternoon dogfight. Stedman was playing Tommy Armour. On an occasion of this significance, the detail both enriched and authenticated the narrative.

From what I gathered, the match was played on a Monday morning when the course was all but deserted. One of Armour's assistants served as his caddy, and one of Stedman's backers, a real estate developer named Frank McCalla, carried his bag.

Stedman must have been nervous at the start, because he bogeyed the first two holes. I could only imagine how his supporters, who knew him as Eddie Brennan, must have felt as Armour parred the first two holes and took an early two-stroke lead. By the turn, however, Stedman had recovered by making three birdies to Armour's one, and the match was tied after nine holes.

Stedman really hit his stride on the more difficult back side, making three more birdies without a bogey to shoot 68 and beat Armour by two strokes. He had defeated the winner of three major championships and had netted $100 over expenses for his efforts.

Chapter 11

IT WAS DIFFICULT for me to imagine how Stedman must have felt after his match with Tommy Armour. Beating a player of that caliber — on his home course no less — was a powerful confirmation of his extraordinary talents.

Jones's notes and the letter from one of the backers describe a golfer with world class abilities. There was no apparent weakness in Stedman's game. He hit full shots long and straight, and he putted well. It was difficult to tell whether he possessed a short game to match his other clubs; he missed so few greens that he rarely was forced to pitch or chip the ball. It seemed to me that Jones was perhaps keeping these notes and other records about Stedman's play so that at least some evidence would exist of this great player.

As things stood now, Stedman had already claimed victories over Jones, Von Elm, and Armour before his twenty-first birthday. No stronger threesome could be found.

But Stedman clearly wanted more. In a letter to Jones, he wrote:

Dear Bob,
I did it! I beat Mr. Amour. He was very nice. Those fellos you sent me to were sur hapy.
This is what makes life worth livin.
Who is nex?
Your friend, Beau

Now that his own competitive days were over, Jones was in a way competing vicariously through Stedman by arranging matches for his powerful protégé that only someone of his stature and influence could. In that respect, it seemed odd that Jones had not personally attended Stedman's match with Armour, but I realized that he probably feared the attention his appearance might draw.

Certainly, the last thing Beau Stedman needed at that time was to draw a crowd. Still, Jones had to be a most interested onlooker, and I wondered if he would eventually succumb to curiosity and find some way to join the gallery at one of Stedman's challenge matches.

Then I remembered what Jones's personal historian, O.B. Keeler, had written about Jones's reasons for retiring. Apparently, competitive golf was a mixed blessing for Jones. Despite his enormous success, which earned him two ticker tape parades down Broadway, Jones found the pressure of competition to be excruciatingly painful. He would often lose as much as ten pounds during the course of a tournament because he was unable to eat.

The weight of public expectations had been great from the time Jones began national competition as a fourteen year old, and it grew heavier and heavier with every passing year. With every triumph, the public expected more. And Jones somehow felt obligated to satisfy them.

It is impossible to imagine the pressure he must have felt in 1930 as he conquered what great sportswriters George Trevor, Grantland Rice, and O.B. Keeler called the "Impregnable Quadrilateral." Yet Jones never wavered and never surrendered to the distractions of the media as his quest for golf's Holy Grail unfolded. When he closed out Eugene V. Homans 8 & 7 to capture the 1930 U.S. Amateur title at Merion Cricket Club for the fourth and final leg of the Grand Slam, Jones completed a year of championship golf unequaled to this day.

Admittedly, there are some who consider Ben Hogan's championship season of 1953 to be a comparable achievement. That was the year Hogan won the Masters, the U.S. Open, and the British Open, and missed the PGA only because it partially conflicted with the British Open. Still, to most golf historians, Jones's victories in the four major championships of his day, all in one year, rank as the ultimate achievement in golf.

At any rate, once Jones had won his Grand Slam, he had no compelling reason to continue to endure the pressures of competition. For Jones, winning the four majors was probably the emotional equivalent of Byron Nelson buying his ranch. The motivation was gone. He had beaten everyone, and he had beaten them often. There was nothing more to prove, and he certainly did not need to endure the intense pressures of competition in order to make a living.

Like Nelson, Jones only made token appearances in competition after his retirement. As the host, he felt obliged to play in the first several Masters tournaments, but the competitive edge of his game was gone, and his performance was, by his standards at least, mediocre.

I could imagine, then, that Jones was having great fun following his young protégé. At last, he could enjoy golf competition without the ulcers.

This was also a time when golf hustling was at its peak. Sending Stedman out to play "money matches" did not take a stroke of genius. All across the country, hustlers like Titanic Thompson were a traveling act. They went from town to town, taking on the local hero at each stop and living off their winnings.

In those days, before Nike and multimillion-dollar equipment contracts, the most a really good player might receive from endorsements was free balls, a new set of clubs, and a little cash each year. Any player who wanted to earn real money outside of tournaments was forced to hustle. That was the reality.

By and large, the only players who chose golf as a profession in that era were those who had no other career options. While golf was played at some colleges, varsity golfers usually graduated to careers in law, medicine, or business, not professional golf. The money just wasn't there.

For Beau Stedman, however, there was no alternative. The only way for him to compete was to hustle. And he had a wonderful friend who was in a position to help him meet — and beat — the best.

The only question was who was next.

Chapter 12

I DIDN'T HAVE TO wait long for the answer. And it was a doozy, to borrow a phrase from that era.

Francis Ouimet was a 20-year-old caddy living with his mother across the street from The Country Club in Brookline, Massachusetts when he stunned the world by winning the 1913 U.S. Open there. And he did so by defeating two heralded British champions, Harry Vardon and Ted Ray, in an 18-hole playoff after the three were tied at the end of regulation play.

U.S. Open history has its share of upset winners, such as Jack Fleck beating Ben Hogan in a playoff to win the 1955 Open at Olympic or Orville Moody winning the 1969 Open at Champions for his only tournament victory as a professional until he found a long putter while playing on the Senior Tour. But no underdog champion has been more celebrated in golf history than Ouimet.

As evidence of the prowess of Vardon and Ray at the time, the dates of the 1913 Open were changed to accommodate their schedules so that they could compete in the championship. Ray was the current British Open champion; Vardon had won five British Open crowns. In contrast, Ouimet, an amateur, had failed in each of the past three years even to qualify for the U.S. Amateur. The only tournament win of any consequence on his golf résumé was the Massachusetts Amateur, which he won a couple of months before the Open at Brookline.

Still, to get to Vardon and Ray, Ouimet had to post a tying score that was better than all other American hopefuls, including a much more prominent young golfer his age named Walter Hagen. Even then, no one seriously expected Ouimet to bear up against the skill and experience of Vardon and Ray in the heat of a playoff.

In the end, however, it was the veterans who faded away while the caddy from across the street refused to yield. At the end of play on that soggy afternoon so long ago, Ouimet had beaten the two favorites by five and six strokes to become the U.S. Open champion. As he was being hoisted onto the shoulders of an admiring crowd, Ouimet turned to his most ardent fan and said calmly, "Thank you, mother. I'll be home soon." He was then literally and figuratively swept away into the annals of golf history.

In reading about all of this, I was becoming as avid about golf history as Cheatwood. The books described Ouimet's victory that day as the event that wrested the crown of golf supremacy from Great Britain for America. It was certainly a watershed for Ouimet personally; he followed his stunning Open victory by winning the U.S. and French Amateur championships the next year.

Like Jones, Ouimet remained a lifelong amateur. He maintained his game at an extremely high level for many years, playing on every Walker Cup team from 1921 to 1936 (including five teams on which Jones was a teammate), and he won his second U.S. Amateur in 1931.

Ouimet resided in the Boston area for the rest of his life, working as an investment broker and executive for the Boston Bruins, the Boston Braves, and the USGA. In 1951, he became the first American Captain of the Royal & Ancient Golf Club of St. Andrews — considered by some to be the highest honor that can be bestowed upon a golfer. Not surprisingly, when the USGA established the Bob Jones Award for distinguished sportsmanship in golf in 1955, it named Francis Ouimet as the first recipient.

So it made sense that Jones would call upon his longtime amateur friend to play Stedman. There was a letter in the file from Jones to Ouimet that told me how it had been arranged.

June 27, 1932
My dear Francis,
It was so good visiting with you on the telephone. You are very gracious to agree to play a match with my young friend. He will be thrilled to meet and compete against the Amateur champion.

As I told you when we spoke, Michael Graham is a marvelous young player. You will enjoy your golf with him. I believe he has the stuff to be a champion, but he played as a professional briefly when he was younger and forfeited his amateur status. He no longer has the desire to follow the professional tour around the country and is content to play the game for fun. (I believe he will, however, agree to a friendly wager on the match.)

I regret that I cannot accept your kind invitation to join you. It would be good to visit with Stella and see your daughters again. Mary would enjoy the trip, too.

Unfortunately, I have to be out West making those golf movies. They insist on putting actors in with me. I only hope I don't end up looking foolish.

Give my best to everyone.

As ever,

Bob

I gleaned from various other notes in the file that Jones even went so far as to arrange for Stedman's travel to Boston. There was a train schedule in the file and a copy of a letter enclosing a check for the fare to a local agent for a ticket in the name of Michael Graham. There was also a note from Stedman, with its customarily poor spelling, thanking Jones. Other notes indicated that the two unlikely allies had discussed the arrangements on the telephone several times.

It was evident that the bond between Stedman and his benefactor was growing stronger. Sitting in my cubicle, I tried to understand the complex dynamics of a relationship that appeared to penetrate barriers of social class, education, and logic. Moreover, it had extended Jones to the very limits of his own ethical bounds, not to mention those of his profession. For what he perceived to be a greater good, Jones had first deceived the authorities and now his own friends.

Being a lawyer, Jones was no doubt familiar with the often-quoted observation by Oliver Wendell Holmes that the life of the law was not logic but experience. Circumstances often transcended rules. There was something about Stedman's circumstances that in Jones's estimation justified his behavior. He did much the same thing with Clifford Roberts. I couldn't help but think that Jones was showing what is now more fashionably called "unconditional love."

It didn't take me long to find out how the match went. As I turned another page in the file, there in front of me was a letter from Ouimet to Jones. It was dated July 15, 1932.

Dear Bob,

It was indeed a pleasure hosting your friend Michael. He was a perfect gentlemen the entire time he was here, and we enjoyed having him in our home, although he appeared overly impressed by it and seemed to find it difficult to relax.

I am afraid the weather was not very cooperative when it came to our golf. I did not think it fair for him to see the course for the first time in our match, so we arranged to play a practice round the day before. We were having quite a heat wave at the time, and even our caddies found the going difficult.

Youth being what it is, I believe your young friend found the conditions more tolerable than I did. Please do not think I am making excuses; I do not believe our match would have gone any differently without the heat.

Michael is every bit as talented as you said. It is a shame that he cannot play in our amateur championships, for he appears to have an ideal competitive temperament. He is very steady on the course and talks very little, as if he prefers to speak with his golf clubs. In fact, he did very little talking during our entire trip and seems to be uncommonly shy.

As you know, our course here is quite long, especially our par fours. Michael's extraordinary length was a great advantage to him, and I found it unnerving to be outdriven by nearly half a football field. I did my best to keep up, however, and was pleased to get around in 73. Still, it was no match for Michael's 70. (In truth, he should have broken 70, but he missed two relatively short putts on the last three holes when the outcome of the match was no longer in doubt. I suspect he was throwing off a bit so as not to embarrass me.)

I would be happy to take up the issue of restoring Michael's amateur status at our next Executive Committee meeting if you wish. As you know, this is becoming quite an issue these days. Much of it depends on how long Michael played professionally. He seemed reluctant to talk about it. If you think he would be interested, however, let me know.

Our best to Mary.

Sincerely,

Francis

In his reply, Jones was brief. He thanked Ouimet for his generosity in hosting young "Michael." As for restoring his amateur status, Jones vaguely indicated that his young friend was not inclined to do so at this time because he lacked the means to join a club and play the amateur circuit. He then wrote, "Michael will certainly be flattered by your offer, and I believe it will encourage him at some future time to apply for a return to amateur competition."

Ouimet's letter must have reminded Jones of the high risk of discovery associated with Stedman's quest. And the betting man in Jones had to know that the odds were against them. For whatever reason, however, Jones seemed determined to help his friend and beat the odds.

Chapter 13

AT THIS POINT I began to wonder how Stedman's opponents were being selected. There did not seem to be any particular pattern involved. Still, I found myself conducting an imaginary roll call of the prominent players of the era and wondering who might be next.

The next match apparently didn't occur for quite some time, until mid-1933. There was nothing in the papers I was reviewing to explain the delay, but persuading world-famous golfers to find a spot in their schedules to play someone they had never heard of was probably a daunting challenge even for Jones.

Then I saw a name I quickly recognized: Gene Sarazen. The man golf writers nicknamed "The Squire." He would be Stedman's next opponent.

I had heard enough about Sarazen to know that he was one of the greats of that era, but I wanted to know more. I hit the books again. It wasn't hard to find an abundance of references securing his place in golf history.

Born Eugenio Saraceni, he became Gene Sarazen when he left the caddie yard to become a professional at the age of 17. He felt his adopted name would be easier for sportswriters to spell and would look better in print.

It wouldn't be long before everyone knew how to spell Gene Sarazen's name. Born within a year of Jones's birth, Sarazen proclaimed his own greatness early in his career by winning the 1922 U.S. Open at Skokie Country Club, beating Jones by a stroke. He quickly showed that winning his first major was not a fluke by adding the PGA Championship in 1922 and 1923, defeating Emmett French and Walter Hagen in the finals. Ten years later, in 1932, Sarazen appended his second U.S. Open title to his résumé, winning at Fresh Meadow, and then won his first British Open crown that same year at Prince's in England. In 1935, Sarazen won the second Masters tournament by tying Craig Wood in dramatic fashion in the fourth round with a double eagle at the par-five fifteenth hole (with Jones in the gallery) and then defeating an astonished Wood the following day in a 36-hole playoff.

Upon capturing The Masters, Sarazen became the first member of one of the most exclusive clubs in all of golf: those players who have won all four of the events now recognized as golf's major championships. Even today, some 65 years or so later, the list of members remains pitifully small; in addition to Sarazen, only Ben Hogan, Jack Nicklaus, and Gary Player have ever been able to display trophies from The Masters, U.S.

Open, British Open, and PGA Championship.

Sarazen's four-wood at the fifteenth hole in 1935 was as much responsible for elevating The Masters to its major championship status as any single stroke ever played at Augusta National. It is still celebrated whenever great golf shots are discussed.

The Masters is alone among the four majors in giving its champions a lifetime invitation to the tournament. Many of its past winners compete well beyond the time when they have any serious chance of winning. Although Sarazen stopped playing in the tournament long ago, it became a Masters tradition for him, Sam Snead, and Byron Nelson to serve as honorary starters. They continued to do so through the 1999 Masters. Two months afterward, the Squire died at the age of 97.

Somehow Jones persuaded Sarazen to play a round with Stedman. In a letter to Sarazen that read much like the earlier letter to Francis Ouimet, Jones promised Sarazen "a challenging match with a young player of great ability." Interestingly, his letter also told Sarazen about the new course he was building in Augusta, Georgia. He described it as "a property with great potential, which I hope can become a winter retreat for all of us to relax and play golf in one another's company." Neither Jones nor Sarazen could possibly have foreseen the roles each would play in making this new course one of the two or three best golf venues in the world, much less that a simple invitational tournament hosted by the club would become a major golf championship on a par with the U.S. Open, the British Open, and the PGA.

Jones's letter to Sarazen was dated July 22, 1933. The match was scheduled for the following August 15. Once again, this would be a "money match," and Stedman's syndicate of "investors" was putting up $1,000. The format this time would be 18 holes at match play, meaning each hole would be a separate contest. The player who won the most holes would be the winner. Apparently Stedman's stock was going up; his share of any winnings this time would be $250.

I had learned a little about match play from watching the Ryder Cup and the U.S. Amateur on television. Of the two formats for golf, match play is older and, in the eyes of many, a much more interesting way to play the game. In stroke play, each player is essentially competing against the golf course. As a consequence, the competitors ordinarily pay little heed to the progress of other players, at least not until perhaps late in the fourth and final round of the tournament. In match play, however, a player becomes very conscious of his opponent, for it doesn't matter how well he plays against par or against the rest of the field. Only his opponent matters. If a player loses his match, he is eliminated from the competition.

The papers I was reading did not disclose the reason Stedman and Sarazen agreed to compete at match play. But it wasn't hard to see why. When two players compete head-to-head, match play is in the eyes of most golf enthusiasts a much better format. If a player meets with disaster on a particular hole, it may mean the end of him in stroke play, but all he has lost in match play is one hole, and he can recover by winning the next hole.

Until 1958, the PGA Championship was conducted at match play. However, while individual match play is preferable for the competitors, it makes for poor television viewing. During stroke play tournaments, at least 60 players remain in the field after the cut, and a television producer can switch viewers quickly from one competitor to the next. Once an individual match play tournament reaches the finals, however, it becomes difficult for television commentators to fill the "dead air" between shots with only two players competing. The PGA changed the format of its championship from match play to 72 holes at stroke play in 1958, which happened to coincide perfectly with the rising success of the telecasts of the Masters tournaments.

All four major championships now have the identical format. Some see that as progress. Others see the abandonment of match play as the loss of golf's purest form of competition. In fact, those who prefer match play are fond of pointing out that par is an American invention. The Scots didn't assign par for any hole because the number of strokes required to complete the hole on a particular day depended on the severity of the weather at the time.

To a Scotsman, the ideal round consisted of getting around the course in "level fours." This produced a total of 72 strokes for 18 holes. Holes playing into the wind often required five strokes, while holes playing downwind might require only three. Thus, while the Scots designated "par for the course" (hence the term), they did not believe that par could be determined for a particular hole without proper regard for the conditions of the day.

It occurred to me that Stedman's match with Sarazen might have been around the time that Sarazen was preparing for the PGA Championship. If so, the match play format made perfect sense.

The match was to be played at the Yale University Golf Club. Stedman would be in for a treat, I thought. One of the books I had been reading was a history of golf course architecture. It described the great courses around the world, and the Yale course was listed.

The Yale course was originally designed by Charles Blair Macdonald, perhaps this country's first great golf architect. Macdonald was the son of a Scottish father and a Canadian mother who was born in Ontario and raised in Chicago. According to what I read, Macdonald first learned to play golf while attending the University of St. Andrews in his father's native Scotland and was able to watch matches involving Old and Young Tom Morris, David Strath, and other great players of the era. After returning to Chicago, he set about promoting the game in this country.

Macdonald's first venture into golf course design was the Chicago Golf Club, which was the first 18-hole course in the United States. In 1895, the Chicago Golf Club became one of five clubs that chartered the United States Golf Association. That same year, Macdonald won the inaugural United States Amateur Championship that was conducted by the USGA. He then moved to New York in 1900 and became a stockbroker while continuing to design golf courses (usually in partnership with Seth Raynor and others) around the country, including such notable venues as St. Louis Country Club, National Golf Links, Sleepy Hollow Golf Club, Greenbrier Golf Club, and the Mid-Ocean Club in Bermuda. Macdonald also wrote a splendid memoir entitled *Scotland's Gift — Golf* and published numerous articles on golf architecture that earned him the unofficial title of "Father of American Golf Course Architecture."

The file I was reading didn't contain much in the way of details about Stedman's match with Sarazen. I was disappointed. Sarazen outlived virtually all of his contemporaries and therefore was the one player from the 1920s with whom I was most familiar. Too, he was universally admired until the day he died, and his record established beyond question that he was an extraordinarily talented player.

Stedman competed in this match as Tom Crandall. If he was intimidated by Sarazen or Yale, it didn't affect his play. He beat Sarazen 2 and 1.

I wanted to know more than the result. My book on golf architecture described the Yale course as having large greens with "deep creases" and "steep banks." I wondered how Sarazen and Crandall nee Stedman negotiated these topographical challenges. Was the match close? Did Sarazen ever lead? How was it decided? Did Sarazen play poorly to lose the match or did Stedman play well to win it? There didn't seem to be anything more in the meager file contents I had before me to sate my curiosity, and I came away from this part of Beau Stedman's story feeling very unsatisfied.

Chapter 14

AT TIMES IT WAS difficult to believe what I was reading. All of this yellowed paper in various forms of newsprint, stationery, legal pad, notepaper, and scraps of envelope backs was yielding a remarkable tale of athletic achievement. According to what I had found, Beauregard Stedman was as good or better than any player who ever lived. Yet the story of his exploits had remained locked away in these scattered file materials for god-knows-how-many years until I found them.

Maybe this didn't rank with discovering King Tut's tomb, but you wouldn't know it from Ken Cheatwood's reaction.

"He hasn't lost yet? Man, what a waste. I hate to think of what-all he might have won. When you can dust off Sarazen on a classic course like Yale, you can start lining 'em up. Take on all comers."

"If anyone was beating him," I said, "I haven't seen it yet." I pointed to a golf encyclopedia that I had borrowed. "Every guy he beat was a big-time player. And he usually played them on their turf."

Cheatwood looked at me. "Do you have any idea how many more matches like this he played?"

I shook my head. "No. It was a year between his matches with Ouimet and Sarazen. Can't play too many at that rate. I wonder why he didn't play more often?"

"That's a good question," my friend replied. "Maybe it wasn't so easy to arrange these things as you think. Maybe Jones was having more trouble than he expected finding 'investors' to back Stedman. You know, they had to be careful about this. There was a price on Stedman's head; he couldn't just come out of the closet whenever he wanted." He paused. "Not to mention the fact that Jones was getting Augusta National off the ground around this time."

I hadn't thought of that. Although Cheatwood didn't mention it, Jones also had his law practice to attend to and his instructional movies as well. There was a lot to this that my ragged assortment of paper wasn't telling.

I just looked at Cheatwood and shrugged. "Only one thing to do. Just keep reading."

My friend put his hand on one of the boxes. "I really wonder what happened to this guy," he said after a while. "People always talk about the 'good old days,' but it wasn't that long ago that life was a lot tougher than it is now. People got lynched for being the wrong color. They got tried and executed because they were the wrong religion or too liberal for the times. Or they got worked to death in sweatshops up north."

Cheatwood's voice had become surprisingly cynical. I couldn't help but notice that there was a passion to it that he usually reserved for our discussions about golf or Greg Maddux. I knew better than to interrupt him, as I expected him to continue.

And he did, asking me, "Have you ever seen old pictures of people in the Oklahoma Dust Bowl? Or in the Appalachians? They look like they're holding on for dear life and don't even know why. Some 'good ole days.'"

Ken's remarks made me realize that the gross injustice of what had happened to Stedman was much more common in those times than I was perhaps willing to admit. Was it any worse because he happened to be a great golfer? What was the real injustice — that Beau Stedman never won a U.S. Open or that he was spending his life in hiding because of a trumped-up murder charge?

I had to wonder whether I was responding more to discovering a great sports story or a terrible injustice. Being a law student, I hoped it was the latter. But, I admitted to myself, I really wasn't as sure as I wanted to be.

Reading on, I found that Stedman's next big match came in the winter of 1934. And it gave him a chance for revenge against the man who had beaten him nearly five years earlier in the Metropolitan Open.

Stedman was going to play The Haig. Walter Hagen. Five-time PGA champion. Four-time British Open champion. U.S.

Open champion in 1914 and 1919. Five-time winner of the Western Open, which was then ranked by many as one of golf's major championships. He won the 1931 Canadian Open, too. You couldn't read a golf encyclopedia or record book that didn't have his name splashed all over it.

Walter Hagen's playing record, as impressive as it was, told only part of the story about his place in golf history. By all accounts, he was a master thespian given to grand dramatic gestures and gamesmanship.

There are those who consider Muhammad Ali to be the greatest showman-athlete of the 20th century. But according to golf historians, he had nothing on Walter Hagen, and he did nothing that Walter Hagen hadn't already done. While Ali may have perfected the athlete as showman, Hagen is widely credited with inventing the role.

In Hagen's day, there was no strict rule about starting play on time. As a result, it seems he thought nothing of arriving at the first tee forty-five minutes late. By this time, his opponent was usually fit to be tied, and any sense of purpose to his round or other semblance of calm was gone. Advantage Hagen.

Hagen would usually compound the felony by pretending not to know — or to care — that he was late. Because he had managed to convince tournament promoters that they needed him more than he needed them, he was usually allowed to play without penalty while his unfortunate playing companion was too distracted to play any kind of decent golf. The tactic worked like a charm — just as Hagen no doubt intended.

Hagen was well off compared to his fellow pro golfers, but that wasn't saying much. He could not have been considered a man of means, but he somehow managed to affect a lavish lifestyle. Another one of his favorite ploys was to arrive at a tournament in a chauffeured limousine, stepping out in a disheveled tuxedo as if he had been out all night. He would then ask his disconcerted opponent — who had been waiting perhaps a half hour for Hagen to arrive — to allow him a few minutes more to change into his golf clothes before they teed off. Of course, Hagen had been to bed early the night before and had spent well over an hour warming up at a nearby golf course, but his opponent didn't know that.

On one occasion, Hagen came to the final hole of a tournament two shots out of the lead. After his drive, he was 150 yards from the green for his second shot on the par-four hole. In order to tie the tournament leader, he needed to hole the shot for an eagle. While an expectant gallery watched, Hagen had his caddy walk to the green and remove the flagstick while he calmly waited in the fairway. Of course, his shot didn't go in, but the headline the next day was about Hagen instead of the poor fellow who won the tournament.

Like Ali, Hagen understood that sports was entertainment. More than any other player of his time, he put on a good show for the fans. It helped, of course, that he truly was a world-class player. For a time, he literally owned the PGA Championship, winning four consecutive times and five titles in seven years.

Although Hagen cultivated his image as a devil-may-care

player, the truth was that he was an avid student of the game and very keenly aware of how to get the most out of his own skills. For instance, he recognized very early in his career that he played much better when he was truly relaxed. To induce the desired state of repose, Hagen developed a pregame routine that he followed religiously. It included a leisurely hour-long hot bath. Thereafter, he forced himself to dress slowly and to do everything at half-speed until he began play.

All of this revealed Hagen to be a far more calculating and thoughtful player than many gave him credit to be. It also meant that this would be a different kind of test for Beau Stedman. Unless he was used to someone coughing in his backswing, jingling change in his pocket as he putted, and inserting a playful needle here and there during the round, he was not going to enjoy competing against Walter Hagen as much as he did his other opponents.

Jones apparently found Hagen hanging out in Florida for the winter. His connections with the Seminole Golf Club at North Palm Beach made it possible for Stedman to take on The Haig at the site of his Southern Amateur win over Jones. At least this time Stedman's opponent would have less of a home court advantage. Some of the club's members, undoubtedly friends and admirers of Jones, became Stedman's backers for this one. Hagen leveraged his bet by acquiring his own sponsors as well.

Seminole was as well-regarded then as it is now. According to my growing library of golf literature (I was becoming as big a collector as Cheatwood), the course had been designed by

Donald Ross in 1929. Ross, of course, was the most prolific golf architect ever, having been credited with the design of hundreds of golf courses in virtually every state in the union. According to published reports, more than 3,000 men were employed annually during the mid-1920s in the construction of Ross-designed golf courses.

From early on, Seminole has enjoyed a national membership that generally has had two things in common: wealth and a low handicap. The course is hard by the Atlantic Ocean, and play has always been heavily influenced by the wind. Seminole is a demanding course with tight fairways and small greens that are heavily bunkered. The length of its holes varies quite a bit, which requires the player to use every club in his bag. As an indication, the length of Seminole's par-threes ranges from 170 yards to 235 yards.

For these reasons, Ben Hogan liked to prepare for The Masters at Seminole. He claimed that playing the course called for great precision in his shotmaking and that, in the course of a round, he was virtually certain to hit every club at least once.

Seminole is also reputed to have the best locker room in the world. However, it is difficult to single out any one thing that makes it so. Photographs of the room do not reveal anything particularly unique about it except perhaps for its size (it is quite large). It is rectangular in shape with lockers against three of the four walls and a bar and shoe shine stand at one end. The ceiling is very tall, perhaps 20 feet high or so, and the middle of the room is occupied by various chairs, tables, and sofas in different seating arrangements. It is, more than anything else, a room exquisitely dedicated to the company of men.

Jones's file contained reports from two of his friends at Seminole about the match. One apologized for failing to ensure that the match attracted no attention, as Jones had apparently requested. Hagen, it seems, did nothing in private. He didn't seem to care who this unknown challenger was and certainly did not fear losing to him. If Hagen was going to play golf, he required an audience.

In the five years since Stedman had competed in the Metropolitan Open, Hagen had competed in 30 to 40 tournaments annually around the world. It seemed unlikely that he would remember Stedman's face, much less his name. After all, he had only seen Stedman that one time.

Still, the other letter to Jones gave evidence of another close call.

Dear Bob,

Your friend Homer Dampf turned out to be every bit the player you represented him to be. He certainly gave Walter all he could handle.

They proved to be quite the opposites in temperament. As you can imagine, Hagen put on quite a show for us and never stopped talking the entire time. Dampf, on the other hand, had virtually nothing to say.

At first, Walter seemed convinced that he had met Dampf before. When they were introduced, he looked hard at Dampf and asked him, "Where do I know you from?" Dampf just looked away, like he was embarrassed. At the time, we thought Hagen had intimidated the poor fellow. If he did, though, it didn't show in the way he played.

Walter started strong and birdied two of the first four holes. Your man came back with two of his own, but Hagen birdied the ninth hole to lead by one at the turn.

Walter stayed hot, making birdies at the tenth and eleventh holes, giving him three in a row, and it seemed that young Homer was done for. However, he matched Hagen's birdie at number twelve to stay only two down and then made birdies himself at fourteen and fifteen to pull even.

His youth showed at sixteen, however, when he tried to cut off too much of the dogleg, found the bunker, and made bogey. Hagen returned the favor at the seventeenth hole when he went for a sucker pin, I suppose trying to make birdie and end the match right there, and dumped it in the bunker. The ball buried, and Walter couldn't get down in two.

They went to the eighteenth all square. As you know, our final hole is a long par four and plays to an elevated green. The pin was front left and much too close to the bunker on that side.

Your man drove first. He hit a prodigious tee shot, but it hooked a bit and ended in the left rough. Walter played it smart and kept his drive on the right side, giving him a far better approach to the flag.

Being away, Hagen hit first. From a clean lie, he hit a magnificent mashie-niblick that dropped next to the pin, bounced twice, and spun back. When it came to rest, he was no more than seven feet away. It was vintage Hagen.

Although Dampf was closer, he had a flyer lie, and it would be difficult to spin the ball. Still, he gave it a mighty effort. The ball flew straight for the flagstick, but flew past about fifteen feet and continued to roll until it reached the very back of the green.

His putt must have been at least forty feet. I thought Walter was going to swallow his cigar when it went in. For the first time all day, his smile seemed a little thin as he faced a do-or-die putt to avoid losing the match.

That was when the showman kicked in. He circled the putt twice. Then he instructed his caddy to do the same. Then they talked with one another. Then he explained to us that the putt looked to break to the left but that he expected the grain to move it to the right.

At one point I looked over at young Mr. Dampf. He had not moved and seemed to be taking it all in with only casual interest. He's a cool customer, that one.

Hagen apparently sensed our growing impatience. Having milked the moment for all he could, he then leaned over the putt and calmly knocked it in without a second glance at the hole.

After eighteen holes, the match was all square.

It was agreed to begin a hole-by-hole playoff on the tenth hole. The first player to win a hole would win the match.

Throughout all this, Homer remained aloof, and we were hesitant to approach him, even to offer encouragement, for fear we would break his concentration. We did, of course, applaud every one of his shots enthusiastically. He occasionally smiled in response, but I am not certain that he ever really heard us.

It ended on the thirteenth hole. As you recall that is one of our best holes, a challenging par three played directly toward the *ocean. Your man had the honor and hit a wondrous shot that bounced right by the hole — we thought for a moment it had gone in — and stopped barely eight feet past. Hagen rose to the challenge and hit one every bit as good, finishing ten feet or so to the left of the flag. His putt slid by just on the right. Homer's putt crept slowly to the hole (much too slowly for us) and appeared almost to stop at the edge before dropping in.*

It had taken twenty-two holes, but we had won our bet. I must say that Hagen was, as always, ever so gracious. Dampf for some reason seemed more anxious to separate himself from the crowd and make a quick departure than to enjoy his triumph.

He is a curious fellow. Not much with the social graces, mind you, but damned near a genius with a golf club in his hands. What do they call them? Idiot savants, I believe. Perhaps that's too strong. He did give us a wonderful afternoon of golf.

All for now. Thanks again.
Tom Wisdom

Like a cat burglar, Stedman had snuck in, claimed another prize, and left without being identified. Although I briefly questioned how Stedman believed he could return to the place where he defeated Jones years earlier and not be recognized, I reminded myself that there was no television in those days. Athletes' faces were not as recognizable as they are now. Stedman's features had rarely if ever appeared in the newspapers or in movie newsreels, so the only people who might have recognized him would have been those who may have watched him play in the Southern Amateur there six years before. Even then, if he shaved or cut his hair differently, it would have been difficult to recognize him as the same person who had defeated Jones. So the few people Stedman may have encountered on the day he played Hagen who may also have seen him years earlier were not likely to put things together.

Chapter 15

IN A SUMMER FULL of surprises, none was bigger than getting to play Augusta National.

Late one Tuesday afternoon, Fred Nathan wandered into the Jones Room and, after surveying my pile of boxes and files in various states of disarray, asked if I could afford to break from my project for a day. I thought he had an actual legal research assignment for me. I allowed that I could. After all, there was nothing particularly pressing about my "busy work."

"Good. Since you're so interested in Bobby Jones, I thought you might like to see the National."

It was apparent from my reaction that I didn't fully understand the invitation.

"You do want to see Augusta National, don't you?"

I couldn't believe my good fortune. I stammered something to indicate my acceptance. I was still thinking I was just going to be taken on a tour of the place when Nathan said, "Good. We'll drive over in the morning, have an early lunch, and tee off around noon."

The thought of playing the site of The Masters had me reeling. Then the worrier inside me spoke up. "How are we getting on? Don't you have to play with a member?"

Nathan laughed. "Daniel Smith is hosting us. I guess you haven't met him yet. He retired four or five years ago, but still keeps his office and comes in most mornings. Dan's our connection."

I remembered seeing the name of Daniel O. Smith on the right side of the firm's letterhead under the heading "Of Counsel." That was a flexible term indicating that a lawyer had some affiliation with a law firm other than as an associate or partner. It was usually reserved for older lawyers who either retired or desired fewer responsibilities than a partner.

After I thanked Nathan again, he took his leave. "We leave at 8:00 sharp in the morning. See you then."

I hadn't relished this astounding development long when I thought of my friend Cheatwood. He would kill to play Augusta National. I was dying to share my good news with him, but I was afraid it might be poor form to do so, like talking to a friend about a party only to find out he wasn't invited.

I was in the middle of this debate when he walked in. One look at his face and I knew he was coming to the party, too. He looked like he had just won the lottery.

"As rush tactics go, this one's over the top," he grinned. "If they want me, they got me."

I agreed it was a pretty impressive move.

He clapped me on the back. "C'mon, we've got to celebrate. Let's go to Clancy's."

Our destination was only a few blocks from the office, well within walking distance. As the name suggested, Clancy's was a bar with an Irish theme. It was in the older part of downtown Atlanta and had somehow avoided demolition even as new buildings had risen all around it. In a landscape of steel, glass, and cement, the wood-and-brick two-story structure that was Clancy's Tavern was an apparent anachronism. Still, it had retained its neighborhood feel and, once inside, patrons felt far removed from the progress that downtown Atlanta had erected all around them.

I loved Clancy's. Walking into the place, I felt transported back in time. Everything was old. I liked that.

I had discovered the place during my first week at work. Through a friend of my girlfriend back in New Orleans, I had sublet an apartment for the summer that was just a block away. One trip to the parking garage next to the office taught me that it was a lot cheaper to walk to work than to pay seven bucks a day to park my car. I also wasted little time in learning the best route to walk to the office, and it took me right past the tavern. I stopped in the second time I walked by after work.

Clancy's was real Irish. No green beer. No cute leprechaun decorations. A sign indicated that it had opened in 1938. It looked like little had changed since then. The paneling had a deep mahogany look that came only after years of polish. The wood floor had been worn deep at the most commonly traveled route around the bar. The bartenders wore white shirts with small black bow ties and white aprons. They rolled their sleeves to the elbow and were constantly wiping off the bar with a damp rag, which they slung over their shoulder while pulling a draft for you.

These were second- and third-generation Americans. There was no thick brogue to be heard when they spoke, but they had genuine Irish roots and a fierce pride about all things Irish.

The most popular brew in the place was a lager called Harp. The most popular basketball team was the Boston Celtics (never mind the Hawks). And, of course, the most popular football team was the Notre Dame Fighting Irish.

They were fierce Catholics as well. Danny Casey, one of the proprietors who was always behind the bar, was quick to tell you, too. I learned early on to leave the topic of Northern Ireland alone.

Cheatwood had also fallen in love with the place. Like me, he preferred its genuine neighborhood feel to the college preppie bars that surrounded the Emory campus.

We found a table in the corner. I started to order a couple of beers, but Cheatwood wanted to celebrate and insisted on two Bushmill's "neat." It had been a long day, and my stomach was nearly empty. It didn't take long for the whiskey to take effect. I knew better than to have another.

If I was happy about playing Augusta National, Cheatwood

was damned close to rapture. He kept drinking, and the more he drank, the more he gushed.

"You know, Augusta's usually closed during the summer. They shut it down about three weeks after The Masters and don't open it back up until around October."

"I hadn't been aware of that," I said.

"Yeah. This is really unusual. Nathan told me they installed some kind of cooling system under the greens to protect the bentgrass in case it gets real hot in April around tournament time. They've had one under twelve for several years, and it worked so well they're installing the same thing under the other greens. Everything's done, so they've opened the course for a couple of weeks to see how the greens stand up to traffic in hot weather. Kind of a test run." He laughed. "Only at Augusta. I guess they figure there's no problem that can't be solved."

That prompted him to begin talking about the golf course. Because the club restricts television coverage to the back nine, most people are unfamiliar with the front side. Somehow, Cheatwood had studied the entire course, though, and began giving me the rundown on each and every hole. By the time he got to Amen Corner, I persuaded him to stop and take a breath long enough to eat something, and we both had stew.

When he finished with his hole-by-hole description of the golf course, Cheatwood began to talk about the history of The Masters. Although I had read quite a bit about the tournament, he was having such a great time that I was content to let him talk. At appropriate intervals, I would punctuate his anecdotes with an agreeable laugh or comment of approval.

Along the way, I began drinking again. Cheatwood never stopped. It was almost midnight when we staggered out of the bar. I have no clear recollection of how either one of us got home.

As a result, the first memory I have of my trip to Augusta National is that I was hung over. Cheatwood, on the other hand, appeared to be clear-eyed and ebullient when we met at eight in the morning. I remember him saying something about big dogs and staying on the porch, but I was in no mood for humor at the moment.

Fred Nathan was next to arrive. He, too, was entirely too chipper for my taste. Fortunately, the coffee I had been pouring down started to kick in, and I was at least able to be sociable.

We made small talk for a few minutes when Daniel O. Smith came walking up. Fred introduced us. I liked him immediately. He was a large man with tanned handsome features. He had an easy manner, and I felt comfortable with him right away.

"Just call me Dan," he said when we were introduced. His tone indicated that he meant it. He was clearly someone who did not stand on ceremony.

We went in Smith's car, which was a four-door Mercedes sedan. It wasn't new; in fact, it looked to be several years old. It appeared that Dan Smith was a practical man who bought a good car and expected it to last.

Augusta is a couple hours' drive east of Atlanta on Interstate

20. The town is located on the eastern border of Georgia, next to the South Carolina state line.

The ride was pleasant. Dan Smith was a gracious host. He wanted to know how we liked our summer. He asked us what we thought of law school and what areas of the law most interested us.

Although I had a hundred questions about Augusta National, I knew from reading about the club that its members were under strict instructions not to discuss anything about the club except The Masters. On rare occasions, a member failed to heed those instructions. Soon thereafter, he became an ex-member with no right of appeal. I didn't want to alienate my host by being too inquisitive.

Augusta National is located on Washington Road on the west side of town. Washington Road is one of the first exits off the interstate as you get into Augusta. Within a minute of turning off the highway, we came upon a large hedge that grew to the very edge of Washington Road on our right. It must have been at least ten feet tall and appeared to be almost as thick. It totally hid from view whatever was on the other side. I was surprised the hedge hadn't been trimmed back by highway authorities as a potential hazard.

I didn't realize that Augusta National was directly on the other side until Dan Smith slowed his car after a half mile or so, just in time to turn into a small break in the hedge. There we were. To our immediate right was a neat and well-maintained guardhouse. In front of us was famed Magnolia Lane. In the distance, at the very end, was the clubhouse. I was looking at something I had seen numerous times in golf magazines.

A guard came out and leaned over to look into the car. His stern expression immediately softened into a smile. "Oh, hello, Mr. Smith. Nice to see you. Kinda different coming out during the summer, isn't it?"

"Yes, it is, Fred. I've got these guests with me today. They're gonna help me test this new system we've been hearing about."

The guard waved us on.

The drive down Magnolia Lane was only 300 yards or so. Trees lined both sides of the drive and formed a canopy overhead. Beyond the trees on each side were immaculately manicured practice areas. The trees were lush and obscured all but the very front of the clubhouse as I looked down Magnolia Lane. When we reached the very end, we turned right into the parking lot.

We piled out of the car and stretched. Caddies appeared and began pulling our clubs out of the trunk. I started to change into my golf spikes, but Dan Smith stopped me.

"We'll do that inside."

I followed him and the others into the clubhouse. As we walked, Smith exchanged pleasantries with the other members he encountered. Judging by the expressions on their faces, Dan Smith was a popular member of the club.

Like Peachtree, the clubhouse at Augusta struck me as more dignified than spectacular. That didn't make it any less impressive. I couldn't say what it was that made the clubhouse seem so distinctive, other than perhaps the fact that this was the clubhouse at Augusta National.

Smith guided us to a smaller locker room upstairs. It had only 40 or so lockers and was virtually deserted except for a single attendant. We changed shoes quickly. As we were leaving, he looked at Ken Cheatwood and me.

"I suppose you're wondering why we came up here just to change our shoes." He gestured around us. "This is the locker room used by past champions for the tournament." With that, he gave us a wink and walked out.

As we visited during the day, I noticed that Smith never referred to the tournament by its familiar name. In fact, I never heard anyone associated with Augusta National use the words "The Masters" during the entire time we were there. It was always called "the tournament."

I had been impressed by the photographs and other memorabilia at Peachtree, but the stuff at Augusta blew me away. First, there was Jones's Calamity Jane putter. And, of course, there were numerous pictures of Jones, as well as some of his golf trophies. But there was so much more.

It is a custom for every Masters champion to donate a club used while playing in the tournament that year. Each club is mounted in a shadow box with the champion's name on it. It made for a rather impressive display.

Then, of course, there were photographs of the members. I immediately recognized the familiar face of then-General Dwight Eisenhower.

As I looked at Eisenhower's picture, Cheatwood told me

that there was a tall pine tree on the left side of the seventeenth fairway that had always frustrated Eisenhower. A chronic slicer, he was forced to aim his tee shot down the left side to give his ball room to curve back to the right in order to stay in the fairway. The tree kept getting in the way.

Finally, Eisenhower complained to Cliff Roberts that he wanted the tree cut down. Roberts refused. Undeterred, Eisenhower supposedly brought it up at a meeting of the members, at which point Roberts promptly adjourned the meeting. The tree has been known ever since as the Eisenhower Tree.

Lunch was simple, but very good. Only three or four tables were occupied. It was obvious that we would have the course mostly to ourselves that afternoon.

After lunch, we ventured back across the parking lot to the practice range. Our caddies were waiting for us, each standing by one of our bags. As I walked to my bag, my caddy held out his hand and introduced himself as Peanut. He said he would be "taking care" of me today. I laughed and told him that might be a bigger job than he thought.

I never slept well after drinking too much, and the previous night was no exception. Although my hangover had worn off, I was still tired. When I swung the club, it felt like I was in slow motion.

I soon noticed, however, that I was making solid contact every time. The fatigue had smoothed out the jagged edges of my swing. There were no more jerks and hitches in it; I was just taking the club back and then following through.

Shot after shot went to the target. Peanut feigned excitement. "We gonna do some good today." I reckoned it wasn't the first time he had used that line on a guest who was eager to be impressed.

We then walked to the pro shop, where Cheatwood and I blew much of our summer's profit on shirts, caps, and numerous other items displaying the prized Masters logo. In all of golf, there is no more prestigious status symbol than the Augusta National Golf Club emblem, and we wanted something to wear back at school that would make our golf-playing classmates jealous.

When we walked out of the other side of the pro shop, I was stunned by the sweeping vista of golf's Garden of Eden that greeted me. Augusta National is probably the most frequently-photographed golf course in the world, but the best photographers on the planet could not have prepared me for the sight of it in person. It was splendid, to say the least.

From the back of the clubhouse and pro shop, the ground swept down into a beautiful valley of perfection that bordered on the surreal. The course deserved its reputation as the best-conditioned in the world; my eyes could not detect a flaw in the entire landscape. Even the color of the grass was richer and deeper than anything I'd ever seen, as if Augusta green had its own chip in nature's paint catalogue. Whoever was superintendent here had to be a first cousin of Mother Nature.

Chapter 16

AS WE GATHERED at the first tee, Dan Smith asked for our handicaps. Nathan was a 12, Cheatwood a 1, and I announced that my handicap was 10.

Dan Smith told us he was a 6. "We'll split the lows." Pulling a coin from his pocket, he turned to Cheatwood. "Ken, call it to pick your partner." He tossed the quarter in the air. Cheatwood called heads. It fell tails.

Smith laughed. "No offense, Fred, but I'll go with youth. Charley and I will take you guys on a one-one-two. Automatic presses at two down." He turned back to Ken. "Since you lost the toss, we'll give you the hill."

The first hole at Augusta is a par four of medium length that is one of the easier holes on the course. However, it's an awkward driving hole. From the tee, the hole bends slightly to the left, but there is a large bunker on that side of the fairway that can be flown only by the longest hitters. There are trees on the left. Thus, while Augusta National is generally an open course, its first hole calls for an uncharacteristically tight tee shot.

Cheatwood's swing was a little quick. He hooked the ball toward the trees on the left, where it settled on the pine needles that are used as ground cover. Nathan hit a short but straight drive. He was in the fairway, but he had a long iron to the green.

Ever the gracious host, Dan Smith gestured for me to hit. I still felt pleasantly tired and not nearly as excited as I thought I would be. My swing was slow and smooth, and the ball flew long and straight down the fairway. Since my game was ordinarily neither long nor straight, I was delighted. I turned to hand the club to Peanut. He gave me a big grin, put the club away, and turned back to his fellow caddies to complete the wager they were negotiating.

Dan Smith lost little time in hitting. He, too, was long and straight, although I suspected he was more accustomed to it than I was. His drive finished 10 yards left of mine. Both of us had seven irons to the green.

I remember very little thereafter about anyone else's round. What happened to me that day had never happened before. Whether I was in what they call "the zone" or was moved by the spirit of Bobby Jones, I played as I had never before played.

My seven iron to the first green was 20 feet from the hole. After replacing my divot, Peanut handed me my putter and smiled.

"Happiness is a long walk with the putter, sir."

I made the putt for a birdie, thanks to a perfect read by Peanut.

The second hole is a downhill par five that is reachable in two, even for me, from the members' tee. However, after another drive down the middle, I pushed my five wood to the right. It finished level with the flagstick but about ten feet or so off the green.

Peanut told me to bump the ball with my sand wedge and let it trickle to the hole. I hit it stiff. Another birdie.

The third hole is a fairly short par four. However, the second shot is uphill to a green that sits on a plateau. It is almost a blind shot, depending on where the flagstick is located. Still swinging slowly and smoothly, I hit a pitching wedge onto the green in regulation and two-putted for par.

The fourth hole is a par three. I hit five-iron to the right rear of the green. My putt for birdie ran past four feet. I told Peanut that I had never putted greens so fast. He told me to keep my backstroke short and aim for the inside right edge. I pushed the putt slightly, but it turned back toward the left at the last second and caught just enough of the right edge of the cup to fall in.

Peanut gave me too much club for my approach to the fifth green. (One thing I learned is that it's always the caddie's fault.) My ball sailed over the green, but fortunately settled in a flat area. I chipped back to within three feet of the cup and made the putt for par.

The sixth hole is the second par three. With the hole located toward the right rear of the green, Peanut said the shot called for another five-iron. I put it in the middle of the green, ran the first putt a foot past, and tapped in for par.

The seventh hole is a par four. Like the third hole, the green sits on top of a hill. A good drive left me with only a nine-iron, but the shallow green left little margin for error, and an unexpected gust of wind knocked my ball down into the bunker guarding the front of the green. Peanut told me to hit my sand shot up the incline that was behind the hole and let the ball trickle back down. I did, and it did. I made a five-footer for par.

The eighth hole is a par five. As with all of Augusta's par fives, it is reachable in two well-played shots from the member's tee. My second shot landed in the fringe, and I two-putted from there for birdie.

I was now three under. I remember vaguely how everyone's attention began turning from the golf course to my score. At first, there were friendly complaints from our opponents about the beating they were taking. When I got to three under, however, everyone began to leave me alone. It was if they knew something special was happening, like teammates avoiding a pitcher in the final stages of a no-hitter.

The sudden silence may have unnerved me. At the par-four ninth hole, I hit my second shot reasonably well, but it finished above the hole. Being above the hole on Augusta National greens is a mortal sin. In most cases, it guarantees a three-putt, because it is impossible to stop the ball near the hole. Despite Peanut's coaching, I could not bring myself to hit the ball as softly as he told me to. It ran 12 feet by the hole. Not surprisingly, I left the comebacker short. Bogey.

Still, I made the turn in 34. For a 10-handicapper, that's climbing awfully high without a net. I was way beyond my customary comfort level.

For some reason, though, I felt strangely serene. The club still felt pleasantly heavy in my hands, and I was still swinging it slowly.

After a short pause at the turn, we headed for the back nine. The tenth hole at Augusta is listed at 485 yards from the back tee. Yet it plays as a par four. The measured distance is deceptive, because the hole runs sharply downhill from the tee with a dogleg turn to the left. Thus, a drive that is struck solidly, especially with a slight draw, will travel well over 300 yards.

The hole is only slightly shorter from the members' tee. I hit a perfect drive, drawing the ball around the corner. Another five iron to the green. My 12-footer for birdie stopped on the lip. For a second, I thought it would fall. No such luck. After waiting the allowed ten seconds, I tapped in for par.

The eleventh hole is another par four featuring a landing area that runs downhill and left. The green is guarded by a pond that wraps around its left side. It's the pond that sank Raymond Floyd's playoff hopes against Nick Faldo in 1990. The flagstick was sitting only 12 feet or so from the left edge of the green.

Handing me a nine iron, Peanut warned me, "Ignore that flag. That's a sucker flag. Hit this to the right side of the green." I did. The ball landed safely. Although I was 30 feet away, it was a flat putt. I lagged it close and again made a short putt for par.

This brought us to the par-three twelfth hole, which may be the most famous at Augusta. It features a narrow green that angles away from the tee. When the flagstick is on the left side of the green, the hole plays to 138 yards. When it's on the right side of the green, the hole plays about 15 yards longer. Club selection is therefore critical, as is evident from the double-digit scores occasionally recorded there at The Masters. The flag that day was on the right. Peanut handed me a seven iron.

I made my first really poor swing of the day, hitting the ground almost an inch behind the ball. It never had a chance to reach the green. As luck would have it however, the ball just cleared the pond in front of the green before dropping in the front bunker.

The bunkers at Augusta are so well-maintained that it's almost impossible to get a bad lie. My ball was sitting up nicely on a slight up slope. As a result, I almost made the bunker shot; the ball lipped out. Another par.

The thirteenth hole is a par five that bends sharply to the left. Rae's Creek and a stand of tall pine trees exact a harsh penalty for anyone who tries to cut off too much of the dogleg. The hole can be reached in two, however, by starting the tee shot down the right side of the fairway with a draw. The ground there slopes back to the left. I made another good swing with my driver, and the ball bounced off the high ridge along the right side of the fairway and ran down to a flat spot 205 yards from the center of the green. I was in the "A" spot for my approach. All I had to do was steer clear of the bunkers on the left. Unfortunately, I overcorrected and pushed my five wood to the right where it caught the meandering portion of Rae's Creek that crosses in front of the green.

I took my penalty drop in an area that left me with a good angle to the pin for my pitch over the creek. I knew the day still had some magic in it when I made a smooth pitch (normally the weakest part of my game) to within eight feet of the hole. Peanut read two balls to the left. It went right in for another par.

The fourteenth hole is a long par four. I pushed my drive to the right again, but the uncommonly generous Augusta fairways gave me plenty of room. Still, it took a full three-iron to reach the green. The trick here is to clear the treacherous mounds on the front part of the green, as they are the most severe on the entire course. The pin was back right, a favorite location for "the tournament." Peanut told me to aim for the center of the green and reminded me that I had plenty of club to get to the back of the green.

I hit the three-iron well, and it finished only a foot or so short of the back fringe. It was a good distance away from the hole, but I had avoided a certain three-putt by getting past the mounds in the front part of the green. In my first big break on the backside, I made the 25-footer for birdie. I was now back to three under.

The fifteenth hole at Augusta is, like its other par fives, reachable in two. It is also like the first hole in that it presents an awkward appearance from the tee. At the time, there was a series of mounds down the right side of the fairway that appeared completely out of place with the landscape, which is flat in the area. (Owing to their artificial appearance, they have since been removed.) To the left is a grove of pine trees. The best drive is down the right side of the fairway, which leaves a clear second shot to the green. Unfortunately, I pulled my drive and came dangerously close to getting hung up in the pine trees. Peanut had gone out to forecaddie and was waiting for me when I got to the ball.

"You got 207 to the front of the green."

I looked toward the green. I didn't like what I saw. It may have been 207 as the crow flies, but I was going to have to hook the ball to get around another cluster of pine trees sitting 75 yards or so down the fairway. I had gotten much too far left. I couldn't afford to come up short, as a large pond fronted the green.

I decided against tempting fate again. I might not be lucky enough to get up and down again. "Give me a nine iron."

Peanut nodded. "Smart play." Whether he believed it or not, he was not about to disagree with me now.

The nine iron finished in the middle of the fairway and left me 85 yards to the flag. It was perfect for an easy sand wedge. Unfortunately, I came up on it a little and caught it thin. It flew to the back of the green before skidding to a stop.

We walked slowly to the green. By now, no one was talking to me. (If they had been, I doubt that I would have heard them.) Peanut read the putt a cup to the right. I hit it on line but too hard. The ball rolled six feet past.

I remember becoming a little irritated for the first time all day. I had done the right thing, played it safe, and laid up. After all that, here I was facing a possible bogey anyway.

I looked over the putt. Then I looked at Peanut. He motioned at the cup with his hand. "Inside left. Don't give the hole away."

He stood off to the side, holding the flagstick. The moment I struck the putt, he said, "You got it!" and began walking to the hole. The ball creased the middle of the cup and fell in. Peanut pulled it out before it came to a complete rest in the bottom of the hole.

The sixteenth hole is, of course, the par three that has seen so much of the great drama of Masters history. Jack Nicklaus sinking a monster 60-footer for birdie in 1975 to steal a green jacket from Tom Weiskopf and Johnny Miller. Corey Pavin knocking it in the water after taking the lead in the final round of the 1986 Masters to dash his hopes. Greg Norman completing his collapse in the 1996 Masters by finding the pond and allowing Nick Faldo to overcome a seven-stroke deficit.

I wasn't thinking of any of that as I stood on the sixteenth tee. But I swear that pond looked like the Atlantic Ocean. And the pin was sitting on top of the ridge that ran along the right side of the green next to a bunker. It was easily the most difficult hole location on that green.

I didn't know whether to hit a six or seven iron, and Peanut seemed to have trouble deciding as well. I didn't think a seven would get there, so we settled on a six. Bad move. I hit the six right at the flag, only it didn't come down until it sailed past the hole into the bunker.

When I got there, my heart sank. I had allowed thoughts of breaking 70 to intrude, which I knew was a mistake. I had read a thousand times how golfers must live in the present. Every article ever published on the mental side of golf had warned against thinking about anything other than the process of playing the stroke at hand. Thinking about consequences inevitably produces tension, and nothing destroys the golf swing like tension.

I did not like what I saw when I got to my ball. The shot would be much too delicate for my fraying nerves. The pin was a mere eight feet from the edge of the green. If I could pitch my ball just clear of the bunker onto the fringe, it still might not stop at the hole. If it rolled past the hole by more than a foot or two, it would quickly run down the ridge and settle 30 or 40 feet away.

Which is precisely what happened. Two putts later, and I had made bogey. Back to two under with two holes to go.

The seventeenth hole may have given Eisenhower fits, but it is really one of the more benign holes at Augusta. I easily avoided the Eisenhower Tree by directing my drive down the right side of the fairway. I was still moving slowly. Peanut offered me a six iron for my approach shot. I wasn't pleased to see the club that had betrayed me on the last hole so soon again, but I took it and made a smooth swing. The ball landed on the green just 14 feet from the hole.

I wanted to make the putt badly. Perhaps too badly. I tensed up, tried to guide the ball, raised my left shoulder, and pushed the putt right. I made the two-footer for par and walked with the group onto the eighteenth tee.

If Eisenhower disliked the drive from the seventeenth tee, he must have loved the eighteenth. Off the tee, the hole falls sharply down to a valley and then takes a sharp dogleg right as it turns uphill toward the clubhouse. There are two large bunkers on the far side of the fairway that are straightaway from the tee. To avoid the bunkers, a player must cut the ball right around the corner. Laying up leaves much too long an approach, and only the longest hitters can launch it over the bunkers across to the tenth fairway. The hole was tailor-made for a slicer like Eisenhower.

I knew I couldn't clear the bunkers, and I wasn't a natural slicer. I would have to try to cut the ball. Opening the face of my driver, I took another slow and smooth swing. The ball slowly began to bend to the right and dropped safely in the fairway. It wasn't very long, but I had a good uphill lie for a three iron to the green.

The flagstick was located that day in the front left portion of the green. It was known as the "Sunday pin placement," meaning that it was traditionally used for the final round of "the tournament." Miss it left, and your ball is collected in a valley that requires a chip up the hill or a lob pitch over it that even Seve Ballesteros wouldn't want. The majority of pros aim for a spot 20 to 25 feet right of the pin in front of the green. That was the spot from which Mark O'Meara made birdie to win the 1998 Masters.

And that was exactly what Peanut told me. "Sucker pin.

Don't fool with that flag. Hit it front right. Easy putt from there."

Ben Hogan supposedly said that a player's golf game is measured by the quality of his misses. By any standards, my three iron to the eighteenth green was as good a miss as I ever hit. I caught it thin, and it came out low. I was sure it wouldn't reach the green, but it landed short and somehow had enough steam to bounce twice before trickling onto the front right side.

We trudged up the hill toward the green. Suddenly I was very tired. Peanut was already talking about the putt. Handing me my putter, he said, "Easy putt. Play it a hole out."

He was either very confident or pretending to be, because when we got to the green he did not even bother to look at the putt. He simply repeated, "One cup to the right. That's the line."

I was nearly 30 feet away. In hindsight, being that far away was the only way I could have made the putt. If I had been within 10 feet, I couldn't have pulled the putter back. From 30 feet, I figured, what the hell, and gave it my best shot.

At first I thought I hadn't gotten it far enough to the right. But it didn't seem to be breaking as sharply to the left as Peanut had predicted. If it held on just a little longer, I thought, it had a chance. It did, catching the left side of the cup. Birdie at eighteen.

I had shot 69 at Augusta.

Suddenly, everyone was pounding on me. The next thing I remember, I was in the clubhouse, and Dan Smith was squiring me around and telling everyone about my score.

They were, of course, the inevitable accusations of sandbagging. As Fred Nathan said, "Whoever heard of a 10-handicapper breaking 70 in his first round at Augusta?"

Even I had to admit it was far-fetched. I do not know what possessed me or induced my calm demeanor that day. Who knows, maybe I owed it all to Peanut. Or maybe there was something else there. Maybe I felt Bobby Jones's spirit that day. He had certainly become a part of me that summer.

Or maybe a part of Beau Stedman had somehow invaded my golfing soul. Whatever it was, it was my 15 minutes of fame, and no one was going to take it away from me.

Chapter 17

I STILL DON'T KNOW if I can explain what happened that day. Perhaps more than any other sport, golf is a game in which such temporary flights of fancy are possible. In fact, I later learned that it is not all that uncommon to hear stories like mine, in which some medium handicapper is relieved of his neurological limitations for a few hours (or even a few days) and inexplicably plays the game at a level far beyond anything he ever experienced before.

In virtually every case, this state of grace is very temporary. To be sure, there are instances in which for some mysterious reason a golfer takes a quantum leap forward and remains there. However, this usually happens after a player has worked very hard to improve and, after months of showing precious little progress, finds that things have come together all at once.

That is a different — and much more understandable —

phenomenon altogether. What happened to me was not the result of long hours of practice. It was, for the most part, serendipitous.

As I thought about it, I had to allow that the combination of alcohol and lack of sleep had something to do with it as well. In some peculiar way, the two factors had combined to slow my golf metabolism and in the process relieve me of the spasms that normally attended my efforts to strike a golf ball. I did not understand much more than that, and I certainly didn't possess the scientific expertise to test my hypothesis.

Anyone who plays golf knows there is a spiritual side to the game. Like baseball, golf is defined by events rather than time. A game of baseball consists of nine innings; a game of golf consists of eighteen holes. Other sports, such as football and basketball, are governed by time. This inevitably changes the pace of the game.

The difference is significant. Games governed by time simply do not allow for meditation on their "inner meaning." Instead, they reward the side that "hustles" the most, meaning the side that plays at the most furious pace. A wide receiver who pauses to reflect on the beauty of a well-manicured playing field is apt to be hammered into next week by a linebacker.

So, I reasoned, if this wasn't some out-of-body experience for which there existed a psychological reason, perhaps it was an out-of-mind experience caused by spiritual forces. However, I wasn't any more of a philosopher than I was a scientist; I had majored in English literature in college. There was nothing in Chaucer's *The Canterbury Tales* or Wallace

Stevens's poetry that helped me here.

Cheatwood wasn't much help, either. First of all, he had shot 80 that day, which for him was a terrible score, and he wasn't in much of a mood to talk about my 69. By all rights, this should have been his 69 instead of mine, and we both knew it. Eventually, though, he came around.

We talked about it one day at lunch. We had gone to a deli about three blocks from work that served an awesome tongue sandwich. It was our third trip that week, but Cheatwood had yet to try the tongue.

"I can't help but think where it came from."

"You eat flank steak, don't you?"

"But it doesn't look the same cooked. I can still tell there's a tongue between those two slices of bread. It's just my nature. I guess I'm not the adventurous type. For me, eating tongue is like hitting driver with out-of-bounds left and water right. I'll hit three-iron every time."

After ordering a Reuben, he turned once again to what was now a familiar topic. "What was your lowest score before that 69?"

"I once had a 74. A couple of 76s. Nothing better than that."

"Well, not many people improve their best score by five strokes, but it does happen. You sure picked a helluva time to do it." He looked off. "Just like I picked a helluva time to shoot 80. The last time I did that in Q-School, I had too many Apollo 13 shots. Signed up to take the LSAT the next day."

I wrinkled my nose in confusion. "What's an 'Apollo 13 shot'?"

He sniffed. "That's where you lose your ball on the dark side of the moon."

I laughed appreciatively.

Turning serious again, he said, "All kidding aside, Charley, I'm happy for you, but I'm so jealous I could spit." He was smiling as he said it, but I knew he was telling the truth.

I checked around, and my friend was right. Shooting a score that much below your previous best was a rare thing, but it did happen on occasion. My 69 was very unusual, but it was not a one-of-a-kind experience.

I played again that very weekend on a nice daily fee course in Marietta called Timber Creek, mainly to see if the magic was still there. Some of it had lingered, but it was clearly fading. I shot 76. While it was six shots below my handicap, it was a long way from 69.

But an experience like that is hard to forget. I continued to think about it virtually every day. Law students are taught to be analytical, and I was having difficulty letting go of this.

As every good player knows, golf is a game of feel. You have to feel the swing, not think your way through it. Thinking produces tension, and tension is a golfer's greatest enemy.

A lot of golfers (myself included) have great difficulty accepting that simple fact. We spend our golfing lives obsessed with the mechanical details of the golf swing — encouraged by the monthly promises of "miracle cures" contained in each new issue of the major golf magazines. Unwilling to accept that there are no Hadacol golf remedies, we run from swing theory to swing theory.

We read Percy Boomer, Ernest Jones, and Tommy Armour. We memorize Ben Hogan's *Five Lessons*. We study Jack

Nicklaus's *Golf My Way*. We watch Hank Haney's videos. And we buy David Leadbetter's swing aids. We respond to every infomercial that promises an overnight solution for our lack of ability. When it's all said and done, however, our handicaps are the same.

In talks with Cheatwood, and in the various books I was reading, I learned that a common thread in the approach taken by good players is to avoid any mechanical thoughts while on the golf course. The place for mechanical thoughts is on the range, where old habits can be discarded and new ones ingrained. When playing in competition, most good players think only about where they want the ball to go. They work on staying confident and loose, knowing that their chances of executing the golf swing well are best if they are relaxed.

I have heard this described in a number of ways. Some players say they stay "out of their own way." Others talk about visualizing each shot by imagining they are watching themselves in a movie. Still others speak of the benefits of a preshot routine that gets them into a quiet state of relaxation. Listen to enough pro golfers, and you get the feeling that many of them can't really tell you why they are so good at this maddening game. Perhaps the best distillation of feel came from Sam Snead, who said he just tried to swing "oily."

As usual, Cheatwood had his own way of putting it. "You can play swing, or you can play golf."

"What's that mean?"

"You ever play basketball?"

"A little." The truth is, I hadn't been all that good at sports.

Lots of desire, but not nearly enough footspeed.

"When you took a shot, did you think about where your elbow was?"

"Of course not."

"No one does. But put a golf club in their hands, and the same guy starts pondering pronation and supination in the middle of his swing. That's okay on the range — if you know what you're doing. But once you step on the golf course, all that matters is where the ball's going. So why think about anything else?"

I couldn't keep it quite that simple. But I did finally realize that I needed to recapture what I was feeling rather than what I was thinking when I shot the 69. That brought me back to alcohol and lack of sleep. It had produced a pleasant tiredness that overcame the tension I usually felt because of my fear of failure. Instead of lashing at the ball, I was too tired that day to do anything other than turn away from it and turn back through it. Rather than trying to hit the ball far, I was just trying to make contact.

I remembered reading stories from touring pros who posted great scores in tournaments when they were feeling too ill to care about anything but getting through the round. They found it difficult to conjure negative swing thoughts when their greatest fear was losing lunch in front of the gallery.

That suggested something to me. While being distracted by a fear of bad results was often disastrous on the golf course, being distracted from thinking about bad results was something else again. Maybe that explained how John Daly could win two majors in the midst of personal struggles with alcoholism and divorce. Perhaps for some, the golf course was the only refuge from negative thoughts and feelings.

However, I wasn't fully satisfied by any of that. I wanted to believe that there was something more to my miracle round. I wasn't ready to go so far as to say that God decided I should break 70 at Augusta, but I did think there was some connection between my inspired play that day and my summer sojourn into the world of Bobby Jones and Beau Stedman. Maybe I had so deeply immersed myself into their lives that some part of them had become part of me.

If I ever wanted to find that wondrous state again, I had to understand it better. Perhaps I would find some answers when I knew more about Beau Stedman.

Chapter 18

BY NOW, THERE were only three weeks or so left in my summer internship. I began to grow concerned about whether I would eventually find the answers to my growing list of questions about Beau Stedman. As I surveyed my cell, I still had a number of boxes to inventory.

The going had gotten slow in the last week or so. I had gotten bogged down in several boxes containing business files. There was nothing in them about Stedman, and it took me a while to get them all indexed and entered in the inventory.

I was just about to take my first break of the day one morning when I suddenly came upon a couple of files that put me back on the scent. Like the earlier files that pertained to Stedman, these were poorly organized, as if Jones himself rather than a secretary had maintained them. Various papers were simply thrown together rather than organized in sections or in chronological order as the law firm files typically were put together.

Among the papers were notes in a handwriting I recognized to be Jones's. They were the most curious entries I had yet to find in this entire improbable saga.

On one aging sheet of paper torn from a legal pad were the following notes:

Beau at the Invitational

1935	(1st rd)	71
	(2nd rd)	68
1936	(3rd rd)	70
1938	(2nd rd)	66
1939	(1st rd)	69
	(2nd rd)	73
1940	(2nd rd)	67
	(4th rd)	69
1941	(3rd rd)	71
1946	(1st rd)	70
1947	(3rd rd)	71
1949	(2nd rd)	68
1950	(1st rd)	71
1951	(3rd rd)	64

I could not believe what I was reading. Had Stedman played in The Masters? If so, how did he pull it off? And why were the scores only for one or two rounds?

I averaged all of his scores. It came to 69.14.

It was a staggering number. I doubted that anyone in the history of the tournament had done as well. Still, it appeared that numerous scores were missing. Maybe Jones was recording only Stedman's good rounds.

I was having difficulty making sense of this new discovery. At lunch, I ran over to the downtown branch of the public library. I was becoming a familiar figure there, as it had a well-stocked section on golf, especially about Jones, Augusta National, and The Masters. I found one that gave a year-by-year history of the tournament, including the scores of every competitor.

I checked for Stedman's name even though I really didn't expect to find it. It wasn't there. I then looked for some of the names he had used in the past. They weren't there, either.

Maybe he used a new name, I thought. I had brought the file with me, and I opened it to the page with Jones's notes on Stedman's "Invitational" scores. Although many of the names of the competitors were unfamiliar to me, I couldn't find a match for the scores that Jones had recorded.

I then decided that Stedman must not have competed in The Masters after all. Maybe Jones's notes were a reference to some other invitational tournament. Perhaps I had incorrectly assumed that his use of the term "Invitational" referred to The Masters because I knew that Jones had preferred to call his tournament the Augusta National Invitational.

Still, the possibility of Stedman competing at Augusta was intriguing, to say the least, and made me realize how well-suited he was for Augusta's course. From all accounts, he had the perfect game for Jones's dream course. He was extremely long off the tee and had a deft touch with the putter. Jones couldn't have designed a more user-friendly track for Stedman.

But entering Stedman at Augusta would have been reckless, to say the least. During the years listed in Jones's notes, the tournament grew in stature and visibility by leaps and bounds. Thanks to Jones's charisma, Sarazen's double eagle, the beautiful setting, and the all-star cast of players, The Masters had caught the media's fancy.

For one thing, sportswriters found sipping mint juleps on the veranda of the clubhouse under the shade of its beautiful trees to be a most pleasant diversion. Jones knew that making the media comfortable was the most certain way to assure that his tournament received excellent coverage, and he provided all the amenities.

To this day, The Masters offers an experience for the media that surpasses the other major championships in golf. Its field starts less than half the number of players as the other majors. As a result, there is far less information to assimilate and compress in dispatches back to the home office. The pace, therefore, is less hectic.

April in Augusta also happens to be a wonderful time of the year, which further adds to the experience. Armed with an unlimited budget, the agronomists on staff at Augusta National seem to have remarkable powers in forcing the azaleas to bloom right at tournament time, not a week before or after. This sometimes requires icing the beds of the plants if the weather is unexpectedly warm before the tournament, but it has always seemed to work.

It also helps that The Masters is the only major championship that is contested at the same site year after year. Members of the media are able to reserve the same house each year and can look forward to familiar surroundings rather than a strange hotel room. They get to know the best bars and restaurants in town and, better still, the best bartenders and waiters. For many members of the Fourth Estate, Augusta is their Capistrano.

All of which meant that sneaking Stedman into the tournament unnoticed would be virtually impossible. While the U.S. Open may have been too bustling for the media to scrutinize some driving range pro from Paducah, Kentucky (unless, of course, he shot 66), the small field at Augusta meant every player would receive at least some measure of media attention. Even though Jones insisted that the field include a fair number of amateurs whose names were unfamiliar to all but a few of the sportswriters who converged on Augusta for the tournament, the job of a reporter was to ask questions. With the scores Stedman was apparently shooting, he was not going to come and go without someone cornering him. Using an alias might buy him some time, but sooner or later someone would check out his story — and blow his cover.

Then there were the other players. It was hard to imagine Stedman on the course driving the ball 300 yards and putting well enough to shoot the scores he did without his playing companions taking notice. Players always check out the competition, and Stedman's scores were likely to put him squarely on their radar screens.

It just didn't make sense. Stedman could not have played at Augusta this often without being discovered. Or could he? If anyone enjoyed a lifelong romance with the media, Jones did. None of them was likely to risk being excluded from the annual party at Augusta by displeasing him or Cliff Roberts. If either Jones or Roberts suggested that a competitor be left alone, there would be few questions asked.

In those days, it was accurate to refer to the group covering Augusta as a sportswriting fraternity. There was a sense of congeniality and professionalism that prevailed among its members, from Grantland Rice on down, and the details of players' personal lives were considered off limits.

Not that sportswriters didn't gossip, of course; that was a big part of the fun. But there was an unwritten rule against publishing such personal information. In short, this was long before the age of trash-talking and tabloids. And no institution was ever more effective at damage control than the Augusta National Golf Club.

In the end, I realized that it wasn't so implausible for Jones to make a place in the tournament field for his special friend and that, if anyone could pull it off by getting the media to look the other way, Jones and Roberts could.

That still didn't explain why the only record of Stedman's scores was Jones's handwritten notes.

Chapter 19

NOT ALL OF JONES'S efforts to pair his friend with other golf champions produced a match. At least that's what I discovered in some papers that included correspondence between Jones and Robert H. Tutwiler, a friend who apparently owned an interest in The Greenbrier in Virginia.

I knew something about The Greenbrier, as my family vacationed there once when I was in high school. Nestled among the Blue Ridge Mountains, The Greenbrier was established at the site of a mountain spring believed to have great medicinal powers. It was also, for a time, the summer home of General Robert E. Lee. The resort features a spa, tennis courts, mountain biking, whitewater rafting, and, of course, golf. In fact it has lots of golf, 54 holes in all.

The nearest town to The Greenbrier is White Sulphur Springs, Virginia. A pretty fair player by the name of Samuel

Jackson Snead grew up in the mountains not far from there. Snead's record is legendary. He won a total of 81 PGA Tour titles, more than anyone else before or since. He won The Masters three times (defeating Ben Hogan in an 18-hole playoff in 1954), the British Open on his first attempt (at St. Andrews, no less) in 1946, and the PGA three times.

According to a media guide from the PGA Tour (Cheatwood's golf library continued to amaze me), Snead also won the Canadian Open three times and the prestigious Western Open twice. In virtually every poll taken on the subject, Snead comes out on top when voters are asked to describe the one player with the most classic golf swing.

Nineteen twelve was a vintage year for golf champions. It produced Snead, Ben Hogan, and Byron Nelson. Other than when Jack Nicklaus was born, no other year can claim to have introduced the world to more major golf championships.

Snead was, of course, a country boy. But he was no country bumpkin. Although he cultivated that image, Snead was far wiser than he let on. A magazine article celebrating Snead's 85th birthday described him as a man who grew up poor and never wanted to be poor again. He managed his money carefully, and he made lots of it hustling golf.

Snead maintained a relationship with The Greenbrier for many years. He was affiliated with the resort in one way or another over his entire career and was a regular presence there. He enjoyed going out on the courses at the resort, introducing himself to guests, and asking if they would like him to play a few holes with them.

The guests were understandably overwhelmed at the prospect of playing golf with Sam Snead and never refused his invitation. They usually didn't learn until later that a charge had been added to their bill for what was described as a "playing lesson." Frequently that lesson consisted of nothing more than Snead advising the guest to use a stronger grip.

Snead also made a lot of money playing exhibitions. Again, he was savvy enough to insist on being paid in cash — and would not tee off until he had the money in hand. Not only was this method of payment less likely to gain the attention of the Internal Revenue Service, but, as Snead often pointed out, cash didn't bounce.

Snead was also game for money matches, provided the stakes were right. He always made sure that he had more to gain than to lose and was willing to let others back him so long as he was promised a healthy share of the winnings.

About the only thing Snead didn't win in his long and illustrious career was the U.S. Open. If anything, it would be more accurate to say that, on more than one occasion, Snead lost the U.S. Open, and none more so than the 1939 Open at Spring Mill outside Philadelphia.

Snead was just entering his prime at the time. Because of his powerful and straight driving, it was always assumed that he would win several Opens before he was done. It was not so much a question of whether Snead would win the Open, but rather how many times he would do it.

According to the records, Snead started the Open in 1939 with a 68. After he followed that with a 71, he was at the top of the leaderboard. In those days, the final two rounds were played on Saturday, and Snead maintained his lead by shooting 73 in the morning round. He continued playing well in the final round, and, with two holes left, he held a commanding three-stroke lead.

At that time, the leaders weren't paired in the final rounds, and there were no leaderboards at every hole as there are now. Later, Snead would say that he believed that he only had a one- or two-shot lead at the time. For whatever reason, he attempted to play the 17th hole aggressively and found the rough, which resulted in a bogey. Believing he was now tied and needed a birdie to avoid an 18-hole playoff with Byron Nelson, Snead pressed and fell out of his wonderfully natural tempo, taking a disastrous triple bogey eight on the final hole when a bogey would have won the Open. He ended up fourth.

In all, Snead had four bridesmaid performances in the Open, finishing second in 1937, 1947, 1949, and 1953. But he always described his collapse at the 1939 Open as the greatest disappointment of his entire career.

Jones had apparently written Tutwiler with a view toward arranging a match between Stedman and Snead. Of course, he did not use Stedman's real name, referring to him as Rudy Sawyer.

Tutwiler's reply was interesting.

August 24, 1947
Dear Bob:
I am sorry it has taken me so long to respond to your letter. As

you know, Sam is out on tour at this time of year. We don't see much of him until the middle of October.

I was able to catch up with him last week, however, by telephone. Perhaps he had had a bad day or wasn't playing well. At any rate, I was disappointed by his reaction to the proposed match.

He had a lot of questions about Mr. Sawyer. I have never known Sam to be reluctant to accept a challenge, but he offered all manner of excuses this time. He also wanted to know what you were up to in sending this fellow to play him.

What it came down to was that he begged off, claiming he was much too busy at the moment to do it. I will approach him again, as several of us here think it would make a great wager. Anyone you recommend is good enough for us. If I can get Sam to change his mind, I'll let you know.

I look forward to seeing you at the club soon.

Fondly,

Robert

If everything I had heard and read about Snead was true, he was not afraid of a challenge. Neither was he likely, however, to dive into a pool without checking its depth. Snead obviously felt he didn't know enough about Rudy Sawyer and wasn't going to agree to play him until he knew what he was getting into.

I wondered if there were other times when Jones was unable to pull off a match. Snead would have been quite a trophy for Stedman. American golf in the forties had any number of great players. In addition to Snead, Hogan, and Nelson, there was Ralph Guldahl, Horton Smith, Jimmy Demaret, Craig Wood, Lawson Little, Lew Worsham, and Lloyd Mangrum. Had any of the others said no, too? Or was Sam Snead the only one immune to Bobby Jones's powers of persuasion?

Chapter 20

As I RUSHED TO complete my summer's work, I discovered that Stedman had in fact finally summoned the nerve to return to Texas, where he had had his close call with the authorities so many years earlier. It was a huge prize that lured him back, and the remarkable reach of Jones's influence was once again apparent.

In the early 1950s developers recognized the enormous potential of an area 50 miles north of Houston dominated by two large lakes, Lake Conroe and Lake Walden. They eventually created several resort properties combining golf, boating, water skiing, and tennis for weekend escapes from the sprawling city to the south.

In the beginning, there was only one decent road out of Houston to the north, and that was U.S. Highway 59. Recognizing the need for better access, the developers per-

suaded federal highway authorities that additional infrastruc-
ture was needed to stimulate economic development between
Houston and Dallas. That led to the construction of Interstate
45. Other highways known as "beltways" and toll roads cir-
cling Houston soon followed. In the 1970s and beyond, the
area north of Houston was the fastest growing in the entire
United States.

The first golf course to be constructed was the Walden Golf
Club. Its developer, John Lundsberg, wisely understood that
his new course had to be bigger and better than the excellent
golf courses in Houston if he expected to attract large numbers of the city's inhabitants. Thus, he commissioned Texas
golf architect Ralph Plummer to find the best section of his
700-acre tract on the South Shore of Lake Walden for his new
golf course.

The result was spectacular. Parts of seven holes bordered the
shoreline, and Plummer utilized the most attractive section of
the property, with changes in elevation that were uncommon
to southeast Texas, to construct a course that was both scenic
and challenging. When he was done, Lundsberg definitely had
a course that was worth the drive out of the city.

Walden Golf Club was set to open on September 15, 1952.
Lundsberg wanted the grand opening to be something all of
Texas would talk about. He came up with a remarkably
grandiose plan. The opening round at Walden would be
played by a foursome of Texas's greatest golf champions: Ben
Hogan, Byron Nelson, Jimmy Demaret, and Jackie Burke, Jr.

Among other things, Lundsberg was a member of Augusta

National. Thus, it came as no surprise to find that he had detailed all of his plans to Jones in several letters. He had also sent Jones the promotional literature he had produced for his property, which included a history of the area and the developer's growth projections. Some of it was obviously intended for investors. While I found it to be interesting reading, I still didn't connect it to Stedman at first.

Apparently, Lundsberg had originally planned to have his friend Jones participate in the development of the resort. Obviously, having Jones associated with the project in some capacity would have great public relations value.

I imagined that Jones received overtures of this kind all the time. However, he was apparently reluctant to become involved with other clubs or ventures because doing so might in some way diminish his relationships with Augusta National and Peachtree.

One of Lundsberg's last letters to Jones indicated that there had been a last-minute hitch in the grand opening. Ben Hogan wasn't going to play. It had been only three years since the automobile accident that nearly killed him, and Hogan was exhausted from his long summer playing schedule. He had advised Lundsberg that, although he would have particularly enjoyed playing with his Texas friends, he felt it best to curtail his activities in favor of rest. Thus, Lundsberg was calling on Jones for assistance in securing a replacement. He was offering an appearance fee of $2,500, which was a sizeable sum at the time.

Lundsberg no doubt expected Jones to produce someone on

the order of Snead. He had to have been surprised at Jones's reply.

September 4, 1952
Dear John,
Thank you for your kind letter. I am sorry that Ben is unable to play, but I certainly understand his need to pace himself these days.

Given the short notice, I am unable to help with the players in whom you expressed interest. However, I do know of a marvelously talented player who would give the rest of your group a fair game. His name is Dylan Heyd. He is an amateur, so you can save your appearance fee. I am sure he would come in return for his travel expenses.

I do not recommend Dylan lightly. He is an outstanding player, and it might make your opening match even more appealing to have an unknown "underdog" match these great professionals shot for shot. I promise you he will hold his own.

I have taken the liberty of speaking with Dylan, and he is available. Just let me know, and I will make the arrangements.
As ever,
Bob

Lundsberg's reply came quickly.

September 7, 1952
Dear Bob,
Received your reply. I love it! It will make great "theater," as

they say. Please make the arrangements.
  Thanks for all your help.
  Sincerely,
  John

Lundsberg clearly had an instinct for promotion. The newspaper clippings that he later sent Jones confirmed that the media liked the angle of the unknown amateur taking on the famous touring pros.

WALDEN GOLF CLUB OPENS WITH EXHIBITION

Special to the Chronicle — The newest, and some say best, of the state's golf courses opened with a bang yesterday on the south shore of Lake Walden. The celebrated Texas trio of Byron Nelson, Jimmy Demaret, and Jackie Burke played the inaugural first round before an appreciative gallery of over 1,000 spectators, but it was a career amateur named Dylan Heyd who stole the show.

Walden is a lengthy course, stretching 6,850 yards. It plays even longer because of changes in elevation, and club selection can be difficult. That was evident throughout the round, as all four golfers misplayed shots because they had misjudged the distance to the flag.

In the end, however, it was Heyd, reportedly recommended by none other than Bob Jones for this exhibition, who made the fewest mistakes. His score of 68 was two better than Nelson and Demaret at 70 and three ahead of Burke at 71. Heyd finished in grand style, making a birdie three at the monstrous 450-yard 18th hole.

According to the resort's public relations director, Camille Harrison, construction on the 135-room hotel adjacent to the course will be complete in six weeks. Plans for a marina are nearly finished, as well as a subdivision featuring lots with frontage on the golf course and on Lake Walden. The golf course will formally open for play to the public on September 23.

There was a picture with the article showing the four players posing with a man identified as Lundsberg. I recognized Dylan Heyd to be Beau Stedman.

Whatever his name, Stedman had claimed three more victims. The magnitude of this achievement was staggering to me; the three players he had beaten were as good as anyone he had faced before.

To begin with, Byron Nelson was one of golf's greatest champions. Even I was familiar with his record. His major championships included the 1939 U.S. Open, the 1940 and 1945 PGA Championships, and the 1937 and 1942 Masters titles. He had amassed a total of 52 career victories on the PGA Tour to rank fifth on the all-time list behind Sam Snead, Jack Nicklaus, Ben Hogan, and Arnold Palmer. That victory total is especially remarkable in view of the fact that Nelson all but retired to his ranch after the 1945 season, when he was barely in his mid-30s.

Of course, Nelson's most spectacular achievement consisted of winning 18 tournaments in 1945, including an unheard-of 11 wins in a row. His scoring average of 68.3 for the year remains the lowest in the history of professional golf. Neither mark, it seems safe to say, will ever be matched.

Jimmy Demaret, the second of Stedman's Texas conquests, wasn't exactly an easy pocket to pick either. For one thing, he won The Masters no less than three times himself. He claimed a number of other tour victories to his credit as well, including the Western Open, the Los Angeles Open, and the Bing Crosby "Clambake."

The third member of the group was Demaret's close friend, Jackie Burke, Jr. Like the others, Burke also had major championships on his résumé, winning both the Masters and the PGA in 1956, and achieved similar success on the pro tour.

Lundsberg wasn't the only one to recognize the potential for golf in the area. Burke and Demaret must have been impressed by what they saw at Walden. Soon after Lundsberg opened his course, they developed and built the Champions Golf Club in northwest Houston, featuring two 18-hole courses they called Jackrabbit and Cypress Creek. As an indication of its enormous respect for the two great players, the USGA awarded Champions the 1969 U.S. Open. Staging the national championship on such a young course (in the Texas heat, no less) was a marked departure from the USGA's historical practice of limiting Open venues to older, historic sites such as Winged Foot, Baltusrol, and Oakmont.

I could only imagine how curious Lundsberg must have been to know about Dylan Heyd. In fact, anyone who witnessed Stedman's exhibitions over the years would naturally have become quite interested in learning more about the remarkably talented player they had seen.

At the same time, I doubted that anyone could have protected Stedman's identity as well as Jones. Just as he deflected inquiries into the machinations of Augusta National by a combination of personal charm and the strength of his reputation, so he also shielded Stedman. It was almost as if Jones could dismiss anyone who was overly curious as prying into things that were none of his business. It was a remarkable power, and he used it well.

At the same time, Jones continued to maintain a fairly meticulous account of Stedman's playing record. I took it to mean he wanted Stedman's achievements preserved for posterity in some way.

It had apparently fallen to me to finish what Jones had started.

Chapter 21

I COULDN'T TELL at first how either Stedman or Jones came to know about Deacon Palmer's boy. Somehow, however, Stedman found his way to Latrobe, Pennsylvania in the summer of 1954 to take him on. At least that's what the file notes I was looking at revealed.

Deke's boy was named Arnold. He had grown up at the Latrobe Country Club, where his father was the pro, superintendent, and general manager. The boy was something of a prodigy. As a ten-year-old, he would park himself on Tuesday mornings at the par-three 7th hole, which required a shot over water, and offer to hit the ladies' tee shots over the water for a nickel.

Of course, Arnold went on to play college golf at Wake Forest and was still an amateur at the age of 24 in 1954. That was the year he won the U.S. Amateur at the Country Club of Detroit.

The Amateur was the first of eight major championships for Arnold Palmer. As most golf fans know, Palmer won The Masters four times, in the alternating years of 1958, 1960, 1962, and 1964, as well as the 1960 U.S. Open, and the 1961 and 1962 British Opens. In all, he claimed 61 professional tournament titles on the PGA Tour alone.

In the process, he became the best-loved golfer of all time. Blessed with enormous charisma, Palmer was perfect for the emerging electronic miracle known as television. Whereas Ben Hogan dissected courses with a surgeon's scalpel, Palmer hacked at them with a machete. It was messy, but effective, mainly because he had a knack for escaping whatever trouble he got himself into. His fearless style of play rendered sportswriters' use of the word "daredevil" a cliché and converted millions of television viewers who had never played the game into golf fans. More than any single player, Palmer is rightly credited with the growth of golf that began in the 1960s. To the media and his fans all over the world, he will always be "the King."

It never occurred to me that Palmer's path might ever cross Stedman's. Then I found a letter from Deacon Palmer to Jones that helped me make sense out of the notes.

July 27, 1954
Dear Mr. Jones,
Thank you so much for your letter of congratulations to my son for winning the Amateur. Needless to say, he was thrilled to receive it and I'm sure will acknowledge your thoughtfulness

with his own note.

I am writing for another reason. Arnold was the first member of our family to attend college. He received a fine education at Wake Forest, but he left early and entered the Coast Guard. He has options that I didn't have, including finishing school on his veteran's benefits and going into business. He seems set, however, on playing professional golf.

Life on tour is difficult. I do not know if Arnold realizes the sacrifices he would have to make, including the loss of a normal family life. He is so confident of his success, however, that he doesn't seem to appreciate the challenge he faces.

You never turned professional, yet you accomplished great things in golf. I think Arnold could do the same. Perhaps he would listen to you. If you would be so kind to visit with him, I would be happy to send him to you.

Thank you.
Sincerely yours,
Deacon Palmer

It was a touching letter. Here was a father who had labored long and hard as a club professional and knew that there was a less glamorous side to professional golf. He wanted more for his son. I reminded myself that this was a time when few professionals had college educations and that professional purses barely offset travel expenses. Most pros traveled together, sharing car and hotel expenses. For this reason, many talented amateurs of the day, such as E. Harvie Ward and Billy Joe Patton, bypassed the pro circuit in favor of more lucrative callings and remained career amateurs.

Deacon Palmer clearly wanted the same for his son. So he was appealing to the greatest career amateur of all time for help.

Jones's reply was thoughtful.

August 2, 1954

Dear Mr. Palmer,

I was pleased to receive your letter of July 27, 1954.

I appreciate your concern for your son. He faces a difficult decision.

I do not know if it would serve much purpose for me to try to dissuade Arnold from turning professional. From what I hear, he is not only talented but has great competitive fire. He might not be happy unless he tries his hand at the tour.

The thrill of winning the Amateur can be intoxicating. As good as he is, Arnold may not fully appreciate how talented other players on the pro tour are. The level of competition among the fellows who play golf every week gets better and better all the time.

Before Arnold gives up his amateur status, I suggest that he play a friend of mine who is a career amateur. His name is Patrick Harris. He is extremely talented — on a level with prominent playing professionals. Playing Patrick may show Arnold that he can remain an amateur and fully test his game (particularly if Patrick beats him).

If you think my suggestion has merit, I will send Patrick to you.

Sincerely yours,
R.T. Jones

Deacon Palmer's reply was short and sweet. It read:

"Great idea! Please put Mr. Harris in touch with us."

Now I understood a handwritten note by Jones that I had encountered earlier in the file. It appeared to be a record of a telephone call from Deacon Palmer. Stedman had shot 70. Young Arnold took two strokes less at 68. If the plan was to discourage Arnold Palmer from turning pro, it clearly failed. Deacon Palmer must have been disappointed.

The note was dated September 8, 1954. As far as I could tell, this was Stedman's first loss since the 1929 Metropolitan Open. He had been undefeated since then in his "matches" with the great golf champions of the day. I felt some disappointment, but it had been a remarkable run nonetheless. No one can win 'em all in golf.

Then I found a letter from Arnold Palmer to Jones. It was dated September 13, 1954.

Dear Mr. Jones,
Thank you for your interest in me and for sending Patrick Harris to play a match. I always enjoy competition, and he is a great player.
My father tells me that you thought Mr. Harris would provide good competition. He certainly did. Dad suggested we play two

days, with two rounds the second day. He said that was the best way to show a player's true ability, and it would give Mr. Harris time to learn the course.

I really thought I had him. I shot 68 the first day and was ahead by two strokes. But Mr. Harris was just getting warmed up. He shot 67 to my 69 the next morning and then really turned it on in the afternoon. I had another 68, but he shot 64, one off our course record. (I had a 63 here two years ago.) Mr. Harris ended up beating me by 3 strokes.

I don't like losing and was pretty disappointed. But Mr. Harris said I have what it takes. He told me not to let anything stand in the way of my dreams. He said he hadn't been able to chase his own dreams and always regretted it.

I know that my father worries that I will be wasting my education. But this is what I want, and I would always wonder what would have happened if I didn't try.

I will remain an amateur so that I can play in next year's Masters as the U.S. Amateur champion. Right after that, I will become a professional.

Thank you again.

Sincerely,

Arnold Palmer

So Beau remained undefeated after all. Jones's note must have been written when Deacon Palmer called him right after the first round. Beau won the battle, but Deacon Palmer lost the war. Still, he lived to see his son become golf's first millionaire and to use his education to construct a business empire that eventually included golf course design and construction, golf equipment, golf clothing, and investments. Wake Forest remains a power in college golf to this day in large part because of a series of scholarships endowed by its most famous golf alumnus.

Like Jones, Arnold Palmer's stature continued to grow long after his competitive days ended. Palmer's last PGA Tour win was the 1973 Bob Hope Chrysler Classic. But his popularity was so great that the PGA Senior Tour was conceived in large part to provide a place for him to continue playing for the public.

That Beau Stedman played a role in all that was one more reason his story had to be told.

Chapter 22

I WAS BECOMING more and more convinced that golf history would never truly be complete if Beau Stedman's story was not told. The very point of an historical record in any sport is to celebrate the accomplishments of its masters so that standards of excellence remain clear. The level of play demonstrated by Stedman over the years was as good or better than anyone who ever played the game.

Besides, he deserved the recognition. I was aware, of course, that there were those who would perhaps disagree. They believed that athletic achievement didn't count unless it had the proper moral tone. It was that kind of thinking that kept Shoeless Joe Jackson and Pete Rose out of Cooperstown.

While I was uncertain of what such a litmus test of athletic morality consisted, it seemed fairly certain that an unresolved murder charge would present a real obstacle to my efforts to secure Beau Stedman's rightful place in golf history. Celebrating the playing exploits of a suspected killer would be a hard sell.

Although I was personally convinced of Stedman's innocence, the fact remained that I had no real evidence to support my convictions. Stedman had Bobby Jones as a character reference (and as character references go, he was hard to beat), but even I knew the difference between that and proof of innocence.

The question was, did he do it? Something obviously made Jones believe that he didn't, but there was nothing in these files to reveal what that was. I would have to have more. I needed something that would show that Stedman didn't do it.

Anyone who watches television knows that the best way for a lawyer to prove his client's innocence is to expose the real culprit. If I was going to be successful in claiming that Stedman didn't murder Mrs. Gladstone, I probably needed to prove who did. It didn't take me long to see that the idea of a first-year law student solving a 70-year-old murder was more than a little absurd.

I had just about resigned myself that there was little I could do to clear Stedman when I found a rather curious file among the last of Jones's papers. It was a genuine legal file, not like the pseudo-legal files that disguised Jones's record of Stedman's exploits.

Jones apparently represented a contractor who had built a golf course on Hilton Head Island many years earlier. The developer ran short of money and conveyed half the mineral rights to the property to the contractor in settlement of his charges. As Hilton Head grew, the golf course became the centerpiece of a successful resort property called Ocean Breakers. When the original owner died many years later, his heirs challenged the validity of the mineral conveyance in the probate proceedings.

I was routinely indexing this file when I saw the name of the original owner: Harold Gladstone.

The probate proceeding had been filed in 1964. By that time, Jones's health was rapidly declining. In fact, I was somewhat surprised that he was handling any legal matters at that point. I could only assume that this was an old client.

Jones's notes indicated that the heirs were the four children of Mr. Gladstone. Given the ages at which they were listed, they would have been very young when their mother died. Jones must have found this as intriguing then as I did now, because he had written questions about life insurance proceeds that Mr. Gladstone had received upon his wife's death.

These proceeds apparently formed the basis for Gladstone's purchase of some 600 undeveloped acres on the island. Although I had no way of knowing whether Mr. Gladstone recognized the potential value of the property, the subsequent history of Hilton Head Island and its explosive growth as a resort destination had made him a very, very wealthy man. In fact, at the time of his death, the probate inventory (which was conservatively valued to avoid estate taxes) listed his wealth at $15 million.

Jones had written Stedman's name next to the note about life insurance. After staring at it a few moments, it dawned on me that the life insurance could have been the motive for Mrs. Gladstone's murder. The obvious suspect, of course, would be the one person who stood to gain financially from Mrs. Gladstone's death — the beneficiary on the policy. That would have been Mr. Gladstone.

Could it be that Mr. Gladstone murdered his wife for the insurance money and then blamed it on Stedman? I quickly read through the rest of the file but found no answer. Instead, the file showed that, immediately after Jones made an inquiry to that effect, the heirs conceded the validity of the mineral conveyance and dropped their claim.

The file included the original papers on the mineral conveyance. I didn't catch it at first, but as I read idly through the documents, I saw the name of Mr. Gladstone's attorney at the time: Henry Montgomery. The selfsame District Attorney who had so eagerly accepted Mr. Gladstone's version of events in 1930 and accused Stedman of the murder. No wonder, I thought, Mr. Montgomery didn't want to look any further or otherwise discover the truth about Mrs. Gladstone's murder. He had a wealthy client who was going to build a major golf resort in Bankens County. Who was he to stand in the way of such progress?

Eventually I realized that, if there was a way to prove Stedman's innocence, it would most likely come from Gladstone's children. I wrote down their names and the addresses listed as they were in the file. Even though the information was over 30 years old, it was a starting point. Hilton Head was only a few hours away. I could drive there and check around. Surely at least one of the children — or some of their children — were still in the area.

There was only one problem. The affairs of a client were confidential. It is the sacred trust of a law firm not to make any of its client's dealings public without permission. All of my "detective" work had been great fun, but it had also been within the confines of the firm's offices. No one had authorized me to go digging around outside of the office.

I needed to share all of this with Ken Cheatwood, as I trusted his judgment. Over lunch, I explained my dilemma. My friend was sympathetic and, as usual, got right to the point.

"Under Georgia law, the attorney-client privilege ends when the client dies. Is this client still living?"

I shrugged. "I don't know. It's a corporation."

"That ought to be easy to check. A corporation only exists if the state recognizes that it exists. The public records at the Georgia Secretary of State's office will show if this corporation is still in existence. If not, it's as if the client has died, and the information in the file is no longer privileged or confidential."

I still saw problems. "Even so, I'm not sure the law firm wants to me to get into all of this."

My buddy wasn't so easily deterred. "Let's cross that bridge when we get to it. First, check and see if the corporation still exists. If it doesn't, let's go see Fred."

I called the Georgia Secretary of State that very afternoon. In typical bureaucratic fashion, I was referred to three different people before someone finally confirmed that the franchise for the construction company had lapsed in 1983. It was no longer a valid corporation in the eyes of Georgia authorities. I requested a certificate confirming that fact, which I paid for out of my own pocket. It arrived in the mail two days later.

It took us over an hour to persuade Fred Nathan to let me go forward with it. At first, he was firmly against it. I believe the reason he eventually relented was because we convinced him that Jones probably would have done it himself if he had not become so ill. I have to give credit to Cheatwood for that pitch. He was going to be a natural as a trial lawyer.

I headed for the Bankens County Courthouse the next morning.

Chapter 23

IT TOOK ALL OF four hours to make the drive to the Bankens County Courthouse, which was located in a small one-McDonald's town called Beaufort. The courthouse wasn't very hard to find; it was located in a square in the middle of town, which indicated that it had probably been the first building provided for in the original plan for the community.

I had left Atlanta at the crack of dawn and arrived at the courthouse by mid-morning. I entered through the main entrance, checked the building directory, and went to the second floor where the conveyance records were located. Starting with the probate judgment transferring the property to Gladstone's heirs, I ran the indices to see if there were any subsequent transactions involving the property.

There were several mortgages placed on the property over the succeeding years to secure loans to the heirs, apparently for the purpose of additional construction or renovations at the resort. In each instance, the full name of the heir was listed, as well as his or her address. By running the records in this manner, I figured to get current addresses on the Gladstone heirs.

I had to hope they were still living. If they were small children when their mother was killed in 1930, they would all be close to either side of 70 by now.

When their father died in 1964, all four children — three sons and a daughter — were still living. The sons were named Benjamin, Bryan, and Michael. The daughter's name was Katharine. She had married a man named Leigh and had subsequently signed all papers in her married name.

Under the terms of Harold Gladstone's will, the four children inherited his entire estate in equal shares. However, the estate had been left in trust, and Henry Montgomery had been named trustee. When he died ten years later, the terms of the trust dictated that the four children select the successor trustee.

It was an unusual arrangement. Ordinarily, the settlor of the trust provided for alternate or successor trustees in the event that the designated trustee was unable to serve. Leaving it to a vote of the beneficiaries only served to invite family conflict.

Seeing Henry Montgomery's name as the initial trustee confirmed my suspicions about his prosecution of Stedman back in 1930. He and Gladstone apparently had a pretty cozy relationship. Gladstone must have seen an opportunity to buy some very attractive land. As the manager of another club on the island, he was more aware than most of the enormous potential to make money by developing additional land on the island. All he needed was capital. The proceeds of a life insurance policy provided a convenient source of funding.

I imagined that Gladstone had recruited Henry Montgomery to be his attorney shortly after Mrs. Gladstone's death. It was possible, too, that he even gave Montgomery a partial interest in his project and promised him additional legal work as he developed his planned resort.

All of that made it very easy for Montgomery to overlook the obvious and focus instead on Gladstone's uncorroborated accusation against Stedman. No wonder Montgomery had been so prickly in response to Jones's letters.

The first mortgage in the records that appeared after Henry Montgomery's death indicated that the trust, which was the proper mortgagor, was now represented by one of the sons, Michael Gladstone. He appeared as the trustee, so he had apparently been elected to that position by his brothers and sister. The mortgage gave Michael's address as 2 Audubon Court, Greenville, South Carolina.

I knew that the conveyance records would probably have a copy of the designation and election of Michael Gladstone as successor trustee. This would be required as evidence to show his authority to enter into subsequent transactions. If I was lucky, the instrument would contain the names and addresses of the other three children to confirm their vote to elect the successor trustee.

And I was right. Turning two more pages in the index, I found an entry showing the election of Michael Gladstone as successor trustee and his authorization to bind the trust in future transactions. I located the instrument in the appropriate conveyance book and took down the addresses of the other three Gladstone heirs. Benjamin Gladstone had a Baltimore address. Bryan Gladstone lived in Charleston. Katharine Gladstone Leigh lived on Hilton Head Island.

I contacted Michael first. It wasn't hard to find him. When I spoke with him, it wasn't hard, either, to figure out why he was the trustee. He was very forceful and direct.

"Why is this any of your business?"

I had to admit it was a perfectly reasonable question. Here I was, a total stranger, asking him about the circumstances under which his father acquired the property that eventually made him and his brothers and sister millionaires.

I didn't know if I could be quite as forthright.

"When your mother was killed in 1930, her murder was never solved. The police claimed that a young man named Beauregard Stedman did it, but they never caught him. Nor did they ever produce any real evidence proving that he did it. I'm a law student, and this has become sort of a project with me. I have reason to believe that Stedman had nothing to do with your mother's death, and I would like to see if I can determine the truth."

Michael Gladstone wasn't buying any of it. He said sharply, "I have no desire to be part of your little project. Kindly let my mother and my father rest in peace." He then hung up on me.

My telephone call to Benjamin Gladstone ended much the same way, and I discovered that Bryan Gladstone had died a few years earlier.

Katharine Leigh was my last chance. Now almost 70, Katharine was the youngest of the four children. In fact, if my math was right, she was just an infant at the time of her mother's murder. According to my notes, Mrs. Leigh actually lived on the resort property. I really had no idea what to expect when I called her.

She sounded pleasant when she answered the telephone. When I told her that I wanted to find the truth about her mother's death, Mrs. Leigh was naturally puzzled. I offered her my well-rehearsed explanation of how my interest in the crime arose. She was not as hostile as her brothers, but clearly somewhat defensive.

We continued to talk, and I felt her defenses begin to weaken. She wanted to know where I was from and what my family did. I knew I had passed that part of the interview when she finally said, "You know, I've always wanted to know what really happened to my mother. I was only three months old when she was killed, so I never really knew her. Her death was something we never were allowed to talk about. I asked my father more than once about it, but he could not stand to discuss it."

Instead of pouncing on the opening, I returned the pleasantries by asking Mrs. Leigh about herself. She told me that she lived in a beach cottage on the property. She was the widow of a Methodist minister, and they had lived in Charleston where he was pastor of First United Methodist Church for 28 years. They had retired to the resort only a few years earlier.

Within just a few months of their arrival, Reverend Leigh developed a nagging cough. When it wouldn't go away, he went to the doctor. It turned out to be lung cancer. He died eight months later.

Mrs. Leigh had apparently not found many people to talk to since her husband died. She didn't mention anything about children, and I didn't feel that I should ask. In any event, she was delighted when I asked to visit her. We agreed to meet the following Saturday.

It was a bright and hot August afternoon when I pulled up in front of Mrs. Leigh's cottage. As I got out of my car, I felt the clemency of the ocean breeze. As slight as it was, the air movement replenished the energy that had been drained by the stagnant air that enveloped the interstate throughout my drive. My clothes were rumpled from the perspiration, but I figured Mrs. Leigh wasn't looking for a fashion show.

She was waiting for me with the door half open by the time I reached her front steps. Wearing a light blue sun dress, Katharine Leigh had a far more youthful appearance than I had expected. She was still pretty, and she welcomed me with a warm smile that put me instantly at ease.

In a pleasant accent familiar to the region, she said, "Come in, Mr. Hunter. You're right on time. I like punctuality in a young person."

She then led me down a central hall to the rear of the cottage, which featured large windows that took full advantage of a wonderful view of the ocean.

"This is extraordinary."

She smiled appreciatively. "Thank you. It is lovely, isn't it? The only bad thing is the work you have to do whenever there's a storm in the area. The house wasn't built with shutters to fit windows this big, so we have to board up the entire rear of the house every time there's a hurricane warning."

"That's a small price to pay, I would think."

She smiled again and looked out at the deep green water. "I can honestly say it never gets old, but it does remind me to appreciate it a little more when I share the view, I must admit."

She pointed to the coffee table between us. "I have coffee or, if you prefer, something cooler."

"Coffee's fine," I said. In front of me was a tray with silver service and demitasse cups. She served me a cup. No matter how hot it was, I always enjoyed fresh coffee.

After the usual pleasantries, she turned to me and said, "So tell me again how you became interested in my mother."

There was something about Mrs. Leigh that seemed familiar. It was as if I already knew her. I remember thinking that she looked like someone I knew, but I just couldn't place who it was. Regardless, I knew I still had to earn her trust. The only way to do that was to be absolutely honest with her. If she suspected me of any deceit, I wouldn't get a second cup of coffee.

"I'm between my first and second years of law school, and I've spent this past summer working as a law clerk for an Atlanta law firm called Butler & Yates. They have me cataloging a bunch of files that belonged to a former partner at the firm who's been dead quite some time. His name was Robert

T. Jones, Jr. He was quite a golfer. You may have heard of him. Most people knew him as Bobby Jones."

I looked at her expectantly. She smiled at me in an indulgent way and said, "Of course I've heard of Bobby Jones. My family's been in the golf business all of my life. You can't help but know who Bobby Jones was. I'm afraid I can't say that I know a lot about him, but I certainly know who he was."

"At one time, Mr. Jones represented a man named Beauregard Stedman. He was the man who was accused of murdering your mother. In looking at the files, however, I couldn't find any evidence that he had done it. Mr. Stedman happened to be a great golfer, too, maybe as good as Mr. Jones. If I can clear his name, perhaps I can get him the recognition that he deserved."

Mrs. Leigh frowned. "I'm a little confused. I didn't think the person who murdered my mother was ever caught."

"That's correct. The District Attorney said your father accused Mr. Stedman of doing it. Mr. Stedman was never arrested or tried. In fact, no one was ever arrested or tried. That's why I'm digging into this. It seems to me that everyone is entitled to the truth."

She seemed puzzled by what I had said. "Why don't you think Mr. Stedman did it?"

I sipped from my coffee cup, mainly to buy some time to organize my thoughts. "In all honesty, I don't have any evidence at this point that he didn't do it. However, Mr. Jones had known him for many years and, from what I read in his files, believed that he was innocent. As far as I know, Mr. Stedman had no motive to hurt your mother."

Ms. Leigh was obviously testing everything I said for credibility. "Having a prominent friend doesn't necessarily make you innocent, now does it?," she sniffed. "Mr. Jones wouldn't be the first person who made a mistake vouching for someone he shouldn't have."

I had to be careful not to argue with her or become her adversary. Instead of challenging her, I treated her question as rhetorical and decided to alter the direction of our conversation. After a long pause, I asked her, "Do you know anything about a life insurance policy on your mother?"

Her reaction was telling. With her cup and saucer in hand, she stood up and walked to the large picture window and stared out at the breaking waves. After drinking what was left in her cup, she turned back to me.

"I knew when you asked to come here that we would reach this point. And if I hadn't wanted to I wouldn't have agreed to see you. But as much as I want to go there, I don't want to go there." She tried to stifle a laugh. "That sounds rather idiotic, doesn't it?"

We were at an obvious critical point. I struggled to find something to say. "There is nothing more personal than family. It's a very emotional issue. It doesn't have to make sense."

"It's a bit frightening to dig things up when they've been buried such a long time."

"Maybe so, but it seems to me that burying a lie doesn't change it into the truth. It's still a lie."

I should have called a two-stroke penalty on myself for

preaching to a woman three times my age. If Mrs. Leigh was offended by my lack of tact, however, she didn't let it show. She seemed to be somewhere else, as if she were thinking of other things.

"I've known about the insurance for a number of years. But every time I asked questions, I got nowhere." She made a sweeping gesture with her arms and said, "I can't tell you where I heard it, but at some point I suspected that this whole place started with money from my mother's life insurance. Something about that has bothered me a long time." She paused. "I wished it had bothered my brothers as much."

I knew I had to keep her talking. "What do you mean?"

"I suppose I've always had this awful fear that what we have came from blood money. You have to understand, my father was a hard man. He was not affectionate toward me. I never was 'daddy's little girl.' He was content to leave me with nannies. And I'm afraid my brothers are a lot like him. I probably would be too, but I was blessed to have a very loving man as a husband for so many years. He taught me another way."

She was now looking directly at me. "And he taught me that no amount of money can wash away the stain of sin."

I liked Mrs. Leigh. And I felt sorry for her. It must have been truly painful living all these years with the nagging suspicion that your father may have killed your mother.

I spoke softly to her. "Mrs. Leigh, I'm just a young law student, and, although I talk a good game, I really don't know all that much about the law, or about anything else, for that matter. And I certainly don't know anything about your mother. But it seems to me that you're entitled to know the truth about what happened to her."

Her eyes were moist with tears. Mine were, too.

My quivering voice surprised me with its emotion as I said, "I can't find the truth without your help."

She bit her lip and didn't speak for a long time. Finally, she stood up. "Come with me. I know where there are some papers you may want to look at."

I followed her outside, and we got into her car. She drove me to the main administration building of the resort. As we walked inside, she said, "It didn't take us long after Daddy died to figure out that we couldn't manage this place ourselves. Mr. Montgomery didn't have the time or energy to do it, either. So we hired an outside company to run things. That's been the arrangement for a number of years. But we still have a lot of Daddy's old records in here."

She took me down a long hallway to a large file room. She walked directly to a large steel filing cabinet, pointed to it, and said, "These were his personal papers. I overheard my brothers talking once, not long after he died. I spent a long time convincing myself I didn't hear what they said, but I guess I just don't have the energy for that kind of rationalizing anymore. There's a good chance you will find something in here that just might clear your golfer's name."

Her voice faltered, and she began trembling. "I think there are papers in here that will tell you that my father killed my mother."

Chapter 24

HAROLD GLADSTONE MUST have been one strange man, but, then, what murderer wasn't. I had heard of people leaving suicide notes. I had heard of people signing confessions. This was a peculiar variation of the two.

Apparently, Gladstone had been diagnosed with terminal prostate cancer in late 1963. He began organizing his affairs, and much of the paperwork in these files related to the creation of the trust for his children.

However, as with any man faced with undisputed medical evidence of his mortality, Gladstone underwent a kind of spiritual transformation. That may have been putting it kindly. What really happened, I suspected, was that Harold Gladstone was worried about going to hell.

So he wrote a long note confessing to a 30-year-old crime. In it, he admitted that he had beaten his wife on many occasions before and that his cruelty toward her probably justified her adultery with young Stedman.

He really didn't blame the boy, either, he wrote. Even after four children, his wife remained a vibrant and attractive woman. Although he hadn't exactly caught them in the act, he could tell something was going on.

Gladstone's note admitted that he couldn't stand the humiliation of a manager's wife taking up with the hired help. So he killed her and accused Stedman of the murder loudly enough to make him skip town. This avoided a criminal investigation, which even in Montgomery's clumsy hands might have stumbled upon the truth.

Of course, Stedman's flight only appeared to confirm his guilt. It also eliminated any immediate need to focus on other suspects.

At first, Mrs. Leigh did not want to look at the papers she was handing me, and she sat quietly as I read them. However, when I was done, she somehow summoned the courage to confront the reality they contained and read them herself.

When she finished, she cried softly for a few minutes. I felt awkward and, after a time, clumsily put my hand on her shoulder. She smiled, patted it as if to reassure me, and said, "My brothers will hate me for this. But I could have no family peace living with this secret anyway. And at least Mr. Stedman's name will finally be cleared. Maybe then at least his family can have some peace."

I had explained to Mrs. Leigh that, if I had evidence of Stedman's innocence, I might be able to carry out Mr. Jones's apparent plan to have him recognized for his golf. She seemed pleased to think that some good would come of this.

I took the note back with me to Atlanta.

I showed it first to Ken Cheatwood. He agreed that it cleared Stedman.

"So Jones was right all along. Our man was framed from the get-go. What a sad story of what might have been."

I nodded. "Think of the championships this man would have won but for this. How many majors would he have taken from others? Jones might not have won the Grand Slam. Hogan might not have won four Opens. Sarazen might not have won all four majors. And what about Nelson's streak? Stedman might have been too old for military service in World War II. What if he had been playing the tour in 1945? There's no way Nelson could have won 11 straight with Stedman out there."

Cheatwood pondered my stream-of-consciousness narrative for a second. "Well, we'll never know, will we? That's the shame of it all."

It didn't take us long to decide what to do next. We took Gladstone's note to Fred Nathan. He claimed to be impressed by my detective work and said I had the instincts to be a good trial lawyer. Coming from Nathan, who had uncompromising standards of excellence, that was high praise.

After allowing me to bask in his praise for a moment, Nathan grew serious and said, "Okay. So Stedman was innocent. After all this time, where do you go from here?"

I shrugged. "I don't really know. I'm sure he's been dead for years, and I don't have a clue how to notify his next of kin, if he has any. I don't think there is any legal action to take. I still would like your permission, though, to do something positive with this."

Nathan looked at me curiously. "What do you mean?"

I looked at Cheatwood and then back at Nathan. "Ken's father has a friend who is a past President of the Georgia State Golf Association. I'd like to find out if there is some way to get Stedman's playing record recognized. He didn't win any major championships, but he beat virtually all of the great players of his time. His story deserves to be told."

I almost winced as I finished speaking. It was not fashionable for law students to be quite so sappy; we were supposed to be fitting ourselves for the cloak of cynicism that veteran lawyers wear so well.

I braced for a put-down. Fred Nathan only smiled.

"Frankly, Charley, I find that admirable. You'll never make a living on that kind of mission of mercy, though. Clearing a dead man's name won't even qualify as pro bono work. You're chasing a ghost, you know that, don't you?"

Neither one of us could call forth any kind of rebuttal to his obviously correct observations.

Instead of showing us the door, however, Nathan looked at us both and asked, "Are you sure that corporation no longer exists?"

We showed him the certificate. He looked at it carefully, even turning over the back. I tried to read his expression but he remained poker-faced. The silence was becoming uncomfortable, as if he was looking for a diplomatic way to tell two of his firm's prized recruits how foolish we were.

His features finally relaxed and, with a trace of a smile, Nathan said, "Well, then, I guess there's no way anyone can say we violated a client's confidences. See what you can do for poor ole Stedman."

We thanked Fred Nathan profusely and left. As Cheatwood and I congratulated ourselves, I realized that I had really begun to like Nathan. To this day, I believe the only reason he didn't say no was because he didn't want to embarrass us or hurt our feelings. He had difficulty admitting it, but he was something of a softie himself. I concluded that Fred Nathan wouldn't be a bad guy to practice law with.

I certainly had better luck convincing him of the importance of bringing Beau Stedman to light than I did with Nicole Chapman, the girl back in New Orleans I had begun dating in law school. She thought I was a little nuts over this whole thing.

"I don't understand. Nothing's going to change. What do you think you're going to accomplish with all this?"

"It's the principle of the thing."

"What principle?"

"There was an injustice. It has to be corrected."

"Why you? No one appointed you to correct this. Don't you have enough going on?"

"It needs to be done. Like Dr. John says, 'If I don't do it, you know somebody else will.'"

"You are so obsessive-compulsive."

"Maybe that's what you like best about me."

We must have repeated that telephone conversation at least a half dozen times over the summer and reached the same stalemate every time.

Chapter 25

I DON'T KNOW what I was expecting the weather in New Jersey to be like, but I was surprised at how cold it was, even for the week after Christmas. I guess I had gotten too used to the South.

At least the snow was fresh and still clean-looking. It was quite a change of pace from New Orleans, which was a balmy 70° when I left Moisant International Airport on Continental Flight 123 to Newark.

It seemed like it took forever for my rented Ford Escort to warm up, but I finally regained full feeling in my hands and feet. I was a little worried about driving in the snow, but Beverly LaFleur at the USGA assured me that I would be fine. The directions she sent me were helpful, too. Every landmark was exactly where she said it would be, and I began to relax as I drove to Far Hills, where the USGA's headquarters are located.

As I motored along, I reflected on the events that had brought me to New Jersey during a time of year when I should have been at home with my family. By the time Fred Nathan had given me the green light on Stedman, my summer with Butler & Yates was almost up. As much as I wanted to pursue Stedman's vindication immediately, I still had a couple of boxes of Jones's files to sort through. That was, after all, my summer work assignment.

I finished indexing the last box around noon on my last day. I then spent the afternoon thanking everyone and trying to gauge the sincerity of their compliments of my work.

I wasn't sure what a first-year law clerk needed to do to rate an invitation to return the following year. The requirements must have been minimal, though, because Fred Nathan let me know that I was welcome to come back next summer. He advised me to stay in touch during the school year.

I had only a week or so after that before classes started again at Tulane, and I spent that time with my family in Birmingham. Although Birmingham wasn't far from Atlanta, I had only been home for a couple of weekends. My parents also visited me in Atlanta once, but that was still less time than I wanted with them. I guess I missed my mother's cooking.

The old saw about law school is that they scared you to death in the first year, worked you to death in the second year, and bored you to death in the third year. My law school career thus far had proved that to be true. I spent most of my first year terrified, and the first semester of my second year definitely was more hectic than anything that had gone before.

My second-year courses were all meaty. That fall I had taken income tax, corporations, evidence, environmental law, and federal courts. There wasn't a weak sister in the bunch. I don't know what possessed me to try to take on so much all at once, but it left me no time to do anything else.

And that included getting Stedman's story before the golf world. Cheatwood's friend in the Georgia State Golf Association had given me the name of Max Humphries, an historian on the faculty of the University of Georgia in Athens who also happened to be a member of the USGA's Museum and Library Committee. I didn't get to call Humphries until sometime in October, when I first came up for air. He was sufficiently intrigued by my story to refer me to Golf House. The staff there was nice but noncommittal. They asked me to submit a proposal in writing.

The last thing I needed was to write an essay on how I had spent my summer vacation. On top of all my course work, I was hard at work on my first case note for the law review, which at that point was in its second rewrite.

Still, it had to be done if the project was going to move forward. It took practically an entire weekend, but I managed to put the whole thing together. The report described how I came to find out about Stedman, how all of the facts were supported by documents in Jones's files, and how this great player was deprived of an opportunity to compete for golf's major championships because of a false murder accusation. I concluded that this was a wrong that the USGA needed to right. That Monday morning, I mailed it to Golf House.

I didn't hear anything for three weeks. During that time, I tried to convince myself that perhaps it wasn't so important for the world to know about Beau Stedman after all. It was my way of preparing for the disappointment I expected in the form of a short and concise rejection letter.

I never did get a letter, however. Instead, I got a telephone call one rainy afternoon in late October (it always seemed to be raining in New Orleans) while I was trying to decipher the various exceptions to the hearsay rule. The caller identified himself as Brett Sullivan. He said he was the curator for the USGA Museum at Golf House.

Sullivan began by apologizing for not getting back to me sooner, but he explained that construction on the new wing of the headquarters had just been completed and everyone was in the midst of moving their offices. "I couldn't get a letter out to my mother right now, much less do business," he laughed. "I don't even know where my computer is. Come to think of it, I can't find my secretary, either."

I liked Sullivan's sense of humor. I wasn't exactly a museum kind of guy and so hadn't known very many curators of museums, but I had expected them to be stuffy. Sullivan was definitely not stuffy, and I was pleased by that.

He seemed excited about telling Stedman's story. In fact, Sullivan suggested that perhaps I hadn't aimed high enough with my proposal. Rather than just publishing an article about my discovery, Sullivan ventured that he was thinking about putting on an exhibition about Stedman's remarkable life in the USGA Museum.

I was flabbergasted.

The USGA's exhibitions, Sullivan assured me (as if I needed assurance), were first-rate. He described a recent one on caddies that had photographs and historical artifacts (some of which originated in the eighteenth century) relating to caddies in Scotland and the United States.

He cautioned me, however, that an exhibition was nothing without good exhibits. Certainly, Jones's notes could be mounted in shadow boxes and placed under glass, and the old newspaper clippings and photographs would be helpful, too. Even so, Sullivan made it clear that he expected it to be a small exhibition. "Better to be small and leave them wishing there were more than to try to make a big deal out of too little."

Fortunately, I had organized and collected all of the Stedman materials in one place before I left Butler & Yates. I suggested to Sullivan that he contact Fred Nathan. He did, and Nathan shipped the materials to him.

Sullivan called me a couple of weeks later. It was early November by this time. "We've just finished sorting through everything," he told me. "We're always interested in anything having to do with Bobby Jones, but the real story is about this fellow Stedman. Jones's personal notes about this guy's golf have been the talk of this place."

Sullivan lamented the lack of photographs or other souvenirs, but indicated that they could "spruce up" the exhibit with numerous pictures from their archives of Jones. He told me he was ordering artwork for large posters detailing Stedman's playing record against the great champions of the past. He also was having a couple of the letters describing the matches enlarged to poster size as well.

Sullivan invited me to come to Golf House. He wanted my personal approval of the layout of the exhibit before announcing a schedule. "This has been your baby, and we want to make sure you're happy with it."

I was touched. Unfortunately, I told him, I was also approaching a nightmarish final exam schedule. That's how we arrived at my coming to Golf House between Christmas and New Year.

My reverie ended when I saw the sign pointing to Golf House. Under its blanket of snow, the USGA headquarters looked like a picture postcard. I regretted not having a camera.

The place was nearly deserted, and I was able to park right next to the front door. As soon as I was inside, I met Sullivan face-to-face for the first time. I'm not sure what I expected him to look like, but I suspect I was looking for someone with a pipe and smoking jacket. Instead, he looked more like a golfer, dressed in a cotton sweater with the USGA insignia and the words "USGA Staff" over the left breast.

He didn't look very happy to see me, however.

Grabbing me by the sleeve, he took me into his office and closed the door.

"I just got served with these this morning." He handed me a sheaf of papers. Reading quickly, I recognized them as the pleadings of a lawsuit. The caption read "Michael Gladstone, et al. versus United States Golf Association."

"What's this?"

"Gladstone's family has sued us. Even got a restraining order. We're shut down until further notice. I tried to reach you before you left, but you were already gone."

I was dumbstruck.

"How can they do this?"

Sullivan managed a half-hearted laugh. "You tell me; you're the one who's in law school."

I looked at the papers again. The petition claimed that the exhibition would cause irreparable injury to the family by falsely accusing Harold Gladstone of murder. It further stated that no court had ever authenticated the documents relied upon by the USGA to assert that Harold Gladstone, not Stedman, was the true murderer of Mrs. Gladstone and that the USGA had no basis to reach the conclusions it did, much less to invade the privacy of the Gladstone family by publishing them to the world.

I looked up at Sullivan again. "According to this, the restraining order only lasts ten days. There's a hearing set then to determine whether it should be kept in place until we can have a full-blown trial on all of this."

Sullivan shrugged. "I'll have to take your word for it. We faxed the papers to our lawyers a couple of hours ago. I expect they'll tell us where to go from here. I'm afraid you came all this way for nothing."

I remembered enough from my civil procedure and remedies courses to know that injunctions were not favored under the law. Judges didn't like issuing them because it was hard to define with certainty what conduct was enjoined. That would be a problem here.

There were First Amendment issues involved, too. Didn't the USGA have the right, if not the duty, to disseminate information about the history of the game? Surely, I thought, it was important to set the record straight. My mind was spotting all kinds of issues, as if this were a question on a law school exam. Unfortunately, this wasn't moot court; it was the real thing.

The upcoming hearing would be crucial. The Gladstones would have the burden to prove to the court's satisfaction that allowing the exhibition would result in the publication of false information that would harm them to such an extent that the damage would be irreparable. This was a fancy way of saying that a suit for money damages after the fact wouldn't be sufficient to repair the harm that would supposedly be done by the exhibition.

It came down to this: If the court believed the Gladstones, Stedman's story would remain buried with him.

Chapter 26

THE LAW OFFICES of Brewer, Czechowski & Newland occupied four floors of the Madison Tower in mid-town Manhattan. While it wasn't a particularly large firm by New York standards, its 100-plus lawyers dwarfed Butler & Yates.

Brewer, Czechowski & Newland had been retained by the USGA to defend the suit brought by the Gladstones. After evaluating the pleadings, the lawyers decided that I was needed as a witness for the hearing. It was scheduled to begin on the following day, which also happened to be the first day of classes for the spring semester.

I was meeting with Steve Wolbrette, who was one of the three lawyers who made up the litigation team for the USGA. Wolbrette appeared to be in his mid-forties. He was not from New York originally; that much I could tell from the way he spoke. I guessed he was from somewhere in the Midwest. He was about 5′ 8″ or so, built like a fireplug, and had the self-assured manner of an experienced trial lawyer who had seen enough combat to know exactly what to expect and how to prepare for it. And, of course, he wore the blue pinstriped suit that was the uniform of every tall-building lawyer.

As Wolbrette showed me into his office, he said agreeably, "They tell me you're a law student at Tulane. Good school. We've got a couple of lawyers from there."

I assumed this was his way of making me feel at ease. I also knew that we weren't there for small talk. I just nodded.

He took my silence as his cue to get down to business.

"Charley, I want to be up front with you. The hearing tomorrow will probably decide whether this exhibition on Beau Stedman will ever see the light of day. The USGA is a nonprofit organization. It likes to spend its money promoting the game, not making lawyers rich."

I must have given Wolbrette a forlorn look, because he quickly forced a smile in an effort to ease my disappointment in what he was saying. "You remember the litigation with Karsten Solheim over the square grooves?"

I did, and said, "That's the case where the USGA grandfathered in square-grooved clubs."

"Right. We always felt we could have won that case, but it would have cost several million dollars to prove our point. Solheim knew it, too. His lawyers flooded us with discovery, and the Executive Committee voted to settle."

Wolbrette looked at me intently. "Brett Sullivan told me what this means to you. Means a lot to him, too. But I have to warn you: Based on past experience, if we don't beat this restraining order at tomorrow's hearing, Golf House is likely to fold on this one."

I understood what he was saying. It made sense that the USGA would prefer to spend its money on junior golf, turfgrass research, equipment testing, and minority recruitment instead of showing that some dead caddie had been denied his place among the legends of the game. Besides, getting involved in controversial litigation only jeopardized its fund-raising efforts.

I understood it, but I didn't like it. In fact, it kinda put me off. While turfgrass research and junior golf were certainly important, so was the USGA's mission to protect the history of the game, I thought.

Wolbrette must have sensed what I was feeling. "Look, I'm not saying that any decision has been made. I just want you to understand how important this hearing is."

I nodded. "I think I understand the issues. They have to satisfy the judge that they're likely to win on the merits and that no other remedy but an injunction will protect their interests."

Wolbrette smiled. "You must have made a good grade in civil pro."

"What happens if we win tomorrow?"

"We hope they quit. If the judge says they're not likely to prevail on the merits, we don't think they'll want to throw good money after bad. After all, the same judge will decide the case on the merits. If she's not impressed with her first look at their case, she's not likely to change her mind later. You've gotta figure they're gonna take their best shot tomorrow."

That made sense.

Wolbrette continued to explain the practicality of our situation. "Besides, if they took it farther and lost the trial on the merits, it would prove you're right once and for all to the entire world. I doubt they want that."

I sighed when he finished. "So it looks like neither side will take this past tomorrow."

Wolbrette nodded in agreement and opened his file as a signal that my preparation for the witness stand was about to begin in earnest.

I could tell he had been through this drill many times before. He handed me a sheet of paper entitled "What to Expect When You Testify." It explained that I would be under oath and obligated to tell the truth. In order to give accurate testimony, it admonished me that it was important to understand each question and to ask for clarification if I didn't.

Wolbrette pointed to the middle of the page. "This is an important point. If you don't know the answer to a question, say so. It's not a test; you don't get points for guessing. Just because you're asked something doesn't mean you're supposed to know the answer. You'll get in trouble if you speculate."

I nodded to indicate that I understood.

"Another thing: Just answer the question. Don't worry about what else they may ask you or answer questions you think they should have asked. Leave that to us." He smiled. "Try to remember: If they ask you the time, you don't need to tell 'em how to make a watch."

I laughed at what must have been an old lawyers' joke.

"We want to keep your direct testimony short and sweet. It'll cut down on their cross. The judge tomorrow is Sarah Bustafani. I don't know her, but I hear she runs a pretty tight ship. We ought to get done in one day."

I was pleased to hear that. I didn't need to miss any more school than necessary.

I did have a question, though. "I'm curious; why'd they sue the USGA in its own backyard?"

Wolbrette pursed his lips. "Good question. It ought to work to our benefit, but from what I hear Judge Bustafani doesn't play golf, so I don't know how much of a home court advantage we'll have."

He held up a stack of photocopies. "I looked into the jurisdictional issue just out of curiosity. These are some of the lead cases. Best I can tell from reading them, we would have had enough to fight them if they had filed in South Carolina, but maybe not enough to win. I guess they didn't want the delays; it would just add to the publicity."

Litigation strategy was new to me, so I was a little reluctant to offer any more observations, but I ventured the comment that it seemed to me that filing the lawsuit would cause just as much publicity as the exhibition.

Wolbrette shrugged his shoulders. "Maybe so. They filed a motion for a protective order to have the proceedings placed under seal. We're researching that issue now. We think the weight of public opinion will be on our side, so we'd like this to be out in the open."

Wolbrette and I spent the next couple of hours walking through my direct examination and covering what we expected the Gladstones' lawyers to ask me on cross-examination. I left his office at mid-afternoon and agreed to meet him early the next morning at the county courthouse in Piscataway.

Chapter 27

WHEN I ARRIVED at the courthouse, Brett Sullivan was waiting for me. After shaking my hand, he led me down a crowded hallway past an interesting cast of characters who were awaiting criminal arraignments. As we walked, he said, "Our courtroom is way on the other end of the building. I was afraid you'd have trouble finding it, so I thought I'd meet you out front."

We then passed the courtroom reserved for Family Court. The people waiting for that court to begin the day's business looked no happier than the criminal defendants we had just passed.

We finally turned down another long hallway and passed beneath a sign that said, "Civil Court." The scenery suddenly changed. The lawyers were dressed better, and so were their clients.

We reached Courtroom D and immediately encountered a

whole cadre of USGA staffers and Executive Committee members. Brett introduced me to a number of people whose names I recognized as some of the leading lights of the golf world. It kind of embarrassed me, to be honest, that they were all gathered together because of some notes I had found in old law files back in Atlanta.

"Looks like I stirred up a whole lot of trouble, Brett. Sorry."

He smiled. "Think nothing of it. If you ask me, this is about the raison d' être of the USGA. What you see is a show of support."

"Yeah, but what will happen to that support if we don't win?"

"Let's play it one stroke at a time for now. We can worry about the rest later."

We found a place to sit in the front row directly behind Steve Wolbrette. As I sat down, I noticed the large seal of the State of New Jersey on the wall behind the bench. The mill-work throughout the courtroom was very impressive and lent a solemn air to the occasion. Some people might have regarded such trappings to be irrelevant, but I couldn't help but feel that they encouraged a sense of decorum and civility that my law professors seemed to believe was fast disappearing from the American legal scene.

At that moment, Judge Bustafani entered the courtroom. She was a fairly attractive woman I guessed to be in her early fifties. And her urgent bearing suggested that she was all business.

In fact, her demeanor immediately reminded me all too much of some of my distaff classmates who wouldn't lighten up during our entire first year of law school. People without a sense of humor often seemed to lack a sense of proportion as well. I didn't know enough about Judge Bustafani to make those kinds of judgments about her just yet, but her serious mien and furrowed brow worried me.

After the bailiff called everyone to order, the judge wasted no time in getting down to business.

"Alright, we're here on number 98-12856, Gladstone et al. versus United States Golf Association. Counsel, please note your appearances."

For the first time, I turned my attention to the other side, in time to see the Gladstones' lawyer rise to address the court.

"May it please the Court, Your Honor, Walter F. Sanders, representing the plaintiffs. We are here today to prevent the infliction of a most serious injury to the children of the late Harold Gladstone, and . . ."

Before he got any further, the judge cut him off at the knees. "I just wanted appearances noted for the record, Mr. Sanders, not opening statements." Her tone was curt. "In fact, after reading the pretrial briefs, I don't believe we need any opening statements at all."

Taking a pencil from a cup in front of her, Judge Bustafani used the eraser end to scratch her head. It was an odd gesture for a woman, I thought. Most women as well groomed as she was wouldn't want eraser shavings messing their coiffure.

I didn't have long to think about that, because Judge Bustafani then turned and nodded toward Wolbrette. "May I assume you represent the defendant?"

Wolbrette stood up. "That's correct, Your Honor. Steve

Wolbrette for the USGA."

"Alright. Gentlemen, we've only allotted one day for this hearing, so we need to make the best use of our time. We can do that if you follow a few simple rules. First, I allow objections, not speeches. There is no jury here, so there is no need to posture. When you have an objection, stand and tell me in a word or two what your ground is. If it's irrelevant or hearsay, say so. Give me credit for knowing something about the rules of evidence."

She paused. "Oh, and one last thing: Don't object that something is 'prejudicial.' You both should know better than that. Everything the other side does is intended to prejudice your case; that's why they do it. But it's allowed unless some rule of evidence prohibits it. So telling me something is 'prejudicial' doesn't help me at all, and I won't sustain any objection made on that basis."

She turned to Sanders. "Counsel, call your first witness."

It was obvious that this hearing was going to proceed at a fast clip. Sanders turned to the man sitting next to him and said, "We call Michael Gladstone to the stand."

A tall, serious looking man rose from his chair and walked toward the witness stand to the right of the bench. His expensive suit, silver hair, and tanned complexion marked him as a patrician. After being sworn, he climbed the three steps to the platform, sat in the chair, and waited confidently for Sanders to begin his questions.

"State your name, please."

"My name is Michael Gladstone."

"And where do you live, Mr. Gladstone?"

"I live in Baltimore."

"Are you the son of the late Harold Gladstone?"

"Yes."

"And your mother was Sylvia Gladstone?"

"Yes."

"When did your mother and father pass away?"

"My mother died in 1930 when I was very young. My father passed away in 1964."

"What was your mother's cause of death?"

"She was murdered."

"By whom?"

Wolbrette was on his feet. "Objection. No foundation."

Judge Bustafani nodded. "That is the heart of the question, isn't it? Mr. Sanders, lay a foundation to show personal knowledge."

"Your Honor, . . ." Bustafani cut Sanders off. "Mr. Sanders, I've ruled. Either lay a foundation that this witness has sufficient personal knowledge to answer your question or move on."

Sanders was apparently a veteran in the courtroom; he regained his composure quickly and turned back to his witness. "Mr. Gladstone, was anyone ever accused of the murder?"

Wolbrette rose again. "Objection. Hearsay."

The judge frowned slightly. "Mr. Wolbrette, you're technically correct. But is there any question here that a man named . . . ," she shuffled through some papers that were in front of her, "Stedman, wasn't it, was accused of killing Mrs. Gladstone?

From what I read in the briefs, that is not in dispute. Let's save our objections for contested issues."

The judge had quickly let both lawyers feel her steel by ruling against each side on successive objections. I wondered if she would continuing going back and forth in this manner, bashing each lawyer with alternating blows. I remembered my evidence professor, Mitchell Johnson, derisively calling judges who did that as "possession arrow judges."

The trace of a smile appeared on Gladstone's face. "A man named Stedman was accused of the murder, but he took off and was never seen again."

"You are aware that the USGA plans an exhibition concerning Mr. Stedman?"

"Yes."

"And that part of that exhibition claims that Mr. Stedman was falsely accused of that crime?"

"Yes."

"And that your father actually committed the crime?"

"Yes."

"Is that true?"

Wolbrette was on his feet again. "Objection. No foundation."

Bustafani had been digging in her hair with the eraser again, which for some reason I found annoying. Her itchy scalp notwithstanding, she stopped in midstroke and frowned at the interruption. It was clear that, once a hearing got started, she didn't like any delays — even for well-founded objections. She turned to the witness. "If you know, Mr. Gladstone."

"It is not true."

Sanders wheeled around triumphantly toward us and said, "Your witness," and briskly walked over to his chair and sat down.

Steve Wolbrette stood up and buttoned his coat. Walking toward the witness, he said, "Mr. Gladstone, did you witness the murder?"

Gladstone sniffed. "Hardly. I was three years old at the time."

"So you don't know who did it."

"I know that my father didn't." His tone bordered on arrogant.

Wolbrette said evenly, "How do you know that?"

"Because he would never have done such a thing."

This time Wolbrette's voice sounded insistent. "But you didn't see who did it, did you?"

Gladstone wasn't giving an inch. "I've already said that."

Wolbrette allowed himself a smile and said, "And since you didn't see the crime, you certainly can't say that Mr. Stedman killed your mother, can you?"

Gladstone shot back, "Why'd he run?"

Wolbrette ignored the question and walked back toward his table. Picking up several pages of paper, he again approached Gladstone, who was almost glowering at him through half-closed eyes. Handing the witness the documents Wolbrette asked in a monotone, "Do you recognize this?"

Gladstone barely looked at the papers before shaking his head. "No."

Wolbrette raised his voice just slightly. "You don't recognize that to be your father's handwritten confession to killing your mother?"

Gladstone barely arched an eyebrow before repeating, "No."

"You don't recognize your own father's handwriting?" Wolbrette now sounded incredulous.

Gladstone gave a slightly theatrical sigh. "My father's health deteriorated badly in the last months of his life. I'm afraid his handwriting became illegible."

"That's not my question," Wolbrette snapped, unable to conceal his impatience with Gladstone's evasiveness. "Do you or do you not recognize this handwriting as being that of your father?"

Gladstone pretended to look at the documents carefully again. "I can't confirm that is my father's handwriting."

"Do you think your sister could confirm whether or not it's your father's handwriting?"

"I don't know. You'll have to ask her."

Wolbrette looked around the courtroom. "Could you point her out for us?"

"She doesn't seem to be here."

Wolbrette was now glaring at the witness. "She's listed as a plaintiff in this lawsuit. Where is she?"

"I'm not sure. She apparently didn't feel up to it today."

Walking toward me and pointing, Wolbrette then asked, "Are you aware that she gave this document to the young man responsible for the story about Mr. Stedman?"

Gladstone continued to play dumb. "I don't know anything about that."

Wolbrette was struggling to hide his disappointment. On such short notice, and without the benefit of depositions, he was having to improvise on his feet, and it was obvious that he was floundering. Cross-examination is all about controlling the witness through prior statements and extraneous evidence. He had neither.

There was nothing to do but surrender. In a voice that showed a trace of his frustration at this turn of events, he said, "No further questions."

Sanders did not bother to redirect. After excusing the witness, he announced in a voice that boomed with confidence that his second witness would be Benjamin Gladstone.

Chapter 28

IT WAS CLEAR WHEN he came forward that Benjamin Gladstone, although a year older, lacked his brother's starch. You could see it in his walk, which was less certain. His eyes gave him away, too. They darted around the room as if looking for something familiar that would relieve his unease.

Sanders walked his second witness through the same well-rehearsed direct examination. He gave an almost verbatim encore of his brother's performance, but it was delivered with less hubris.

Wolbrette knew that Benjamin Gladstone had seen and heard his cross-examination of his brother and no doubt would attempt to mimic his answers if asked the same questions. He also picked up on Benjamin's less confident demeanor. So he changed things up a bit.

"Mr. Gladstone, where is your sister today?"

The witness looked over at his lawyer, as if seeking assistance in answering the question. However, Wolbrette was having none of that. He stepped into the witness's line of vision to Sanders and asked in an almost grating voice, "Why are you looking at Mr. Sanders, Mr. Gladstone? Do you think he knows where his other client is?"

Sanders rose to the bait. "Objection! That's uncalled for."

Bustafani couldn't resist a smile. She had seen lawyers gambol with one another in this manner many, many times. "I can't find 'uncalled for' in my evidence book, counselor."

Well, then, it's a compound question, Judge." Sanders was too experienced not to recover quickly.

She pointed her eraser tip at Sanders. "That one I recognize. Sustained."

Wolbrette got back on track. "Where is your sister, Mr. Gladstone?"

"I'm not sure," he said, a little uncertainly.

Wolbrette must have sensed his weakness and leaned in to press for details. The surest way to expose a lie was to make the witness elaborate. They usually tripped themselves up one way or the other. "When did you last speak with her?"

The eldest of the Gladstone siblings shifted uneasily in his chair. "It's been awhile."

How long ago?" Wolbrette was asking his questions quickly, trying to impose a cadence on his interrogation that would leave the witness little time to think before answering.

"I don't remember exactly."

It was a subtle thing, but the USGA lawyer sensed that the

witness was about to give up the lie, so he quickly asked, "Well, you filed this lawsuit less than two weeks ago. Does that help pinpoint a time?"

Benjamin Gladstone was growing noticeably more uncomfortable. "I, uh, I really don't know."

Wolbrette pressed him again. "Well, what did you talk about when you last spoke with her?"

Sanders couldn't stand it any more. His witness was in trouble, and he knew it. He was quickly on his feet. "Objection, Your Honor. Calls for disclosure of privileged communications."

Bustafani wrinkled her nose. Tapping the eraser end of her pencil on the evidence code that rested next to her water pitcher, she asked sardonically, "Are you claiming some kind of a brother-sister privilege here, counselor?"

"No, Your Honor. Attorney-client if those conversations occurred in my presence."

"I think we understand that Mr. Wolbrette was not asking about that. Overruled."

Sanders's objection had served its purpose, however. The break in the action had allowed Benjamin Gladstone to regain his composure, if ever so slightly.

He sat up straight and looked at Wolbrette. "What was your question again?"

"What did you talk about the last time you spoke with your sister Katharine?"

"I really don't remember. Small talk, mostly."

"Where was she at the time?"

Gladstone tried to appear thoughtful. "I believe we talked

on the telephone. She was probably at her home."

Wolbrette then looked around the courtroom and threw up his arms in a mocking way. "And you don't know where she is today?"

"Objection. Asked and answered."

"Sustained."

Wolbrette's tone grew more sarcastic. "And you don't know what could have been so important as to keep her from this hearing?"

"Objection. Argumentative."

"Sustained."

Wolbrette dropped his pencil on the table in front of him in disgust. "No further questions."

We took a short recess. I approached Wolbrette in the hall. "Why didn't you ask Benjamin Gladstone about his father's handwriting?" It seemed to be an obvious question to me.

Wolbrette shook his head. "He would only have repeated what his brother said. You don't win by proving the other side's case. Let the judge wonder why Katharine isn't here."

"Well, how are we going to prove that the confession was written by Harold Gladstone?"

Wolbrette smiled. "That's where you come in."

When court reconvened, Sanders declined Bustafani's invitation to call his next witness by declaring, "We rest, Your Honor."

Wolbrette seemed surprised. The Gladstones had the burden of proof. This meant that they had to produce enough evidence to persuade the judge that their claims were more likely than not true.

Wolbrette stood up and moved for a directed verdict, claiming that the plaintiffs had not made a sufficient showing to move forward with the case.

Bustafani began shaking her head in disagreement before Wolbrette finished speaking. Tapping her desk with the ever-present pencil, she said, "They deny the confession was made by their father. There's no evidence it was. Motion denied. Call your first witness."

"Charles Hunter."

I didn't know I was going on first. The next thing I knew, I was seated on the witness stand, a lot closer to Judge Bustafani and her bad hair day than I wanted to be. In fact, the whole thing happened so quickly that I don't even remember being sworn.

I do recall seeing Wolbrette walking toward me holding the confession in his hand. He presented it to me and said, "Do you recognize this?"

"Yes."

"When did you first see it?"

"Mrs. Leigh gave it to me last summer."

"Did she tell you what it was?"

Sanders rose quickly from his chair. "Objection. Hearsay."

The judge barely gave it a thought before ruling. "Sustained."

Wolbrette spun around in surprise. "Judge, Mrs. Leigh is a party. It's an admission against interest, which is not hearsay."

Bustafani wouldn't budge. "I said sustained." She pulled out her eraser again and pointed it at him. "Now, ask your next question, Mr. Wolbrette."

He turned back to me. I could tell he was upset. "Do you know who wrote this?"

"Yes."

"Who wrote it?"

Sanders was on his feet again. "Objection, Your Honor. He's just going through the back door. The answer has to be based on hearsay."

Bustafani looked at Wolbrette. "Lay a foundation for personal knowledge."

"Judge, the witness was given this document by Katharine Leigh. Anything she said about it is admissible. Like I said before, it's an admission."

Judge Bustafani clearly didn't like being questioned about her decisions. "Mr. Wolbrette, I've ruled. If you can't lay a foundation to show that this witness has personal knowledge concerning who wrote this document, he can't testify any further about it."

Wolbrette shook his head. "Judge, the one person who can supply that information isn't here."

She responded by asking pointedly, "Do you have information that Mrs. Leigh has been hidden away by Mr. Sanders or the other plaintiffs?"

Wolbrette shook his head. "No."

"Did you try to subpoena her?"

Wolbrette tried to look surprised at her question. "No, we didn't think it would be necessary."

Bustafani was insistent. "Do you know for a fact that Mrs.

Leigh can identify the author of that document?"

Wolbrette seemed helpless at the moment. "No, Your Honor, but..."

She leaned back in her chair and tapped her cheek with the pencil. "Mr. Wolbrette, we're wasting time here. Call your next witness."

The USGA lawyer looked beat. "May we have a brief recess to decide who our remaining witnesses will be?"

Bustafani was clearly irritated by the request even though it was necessitated by her unexpected evidentiary rulings. "We'll never get done if we take a break every five minutes. I expected you to be prepared for this hearing, Mr. Wolbrette. You've got three minutes. Get your ducks in a row or I'll consider you to have rested your case, and I'll rule from the bench."

We huddled in the back of the courtroom. I knew from my evidence class that what Katharine Leigh told me was admissible. I should have been allowed to testify that she had told me the note was in her father's handwriting. According to what I had learned during the just-completed semester, the judge was dead wrong to exclude it.

In a stage whisper, I said to our slightly crestfallen lawyer, "Katharine Leigh is one of the plaintiffs. Statements by adverse parties are not even defined as hearsay under the rules."

Wolbrette gave me a tired smile. "I know that, Charley."

I still failed to appreciate the futility of our situation. "Well, isn't that reversible error?"

Wolbrette said with a noticeable effort to be patient, "If the court of appeal doesn't dismiss it as harmless error. Anyway, it doesn't matter if we don't appeal, does it?"

"So where do we go from here?"

Wolbrette shook his head. "Without someone identifying that handwriting as Harold Gladstone's, we go down."

My heart sank. I hadn't ever considered that the Gladstone family might not be eager to let the world know that their father killed their mother — even though it meant clearing an innocent man.

But, of course, to their way of thinking, this supposedly innocent man was dead. Why should they want to wash their dirty linen before the world when it wouldn't help a single living soul? It was an easy way to rationalize their position.

I found it hard to believe it could end this way, but at that moment I felt I should have seen it coming.

The sound of Judge Bustafani reentering the courtroom signaled that we were to return to our seats. The judge climbed onto the bench, seated herself ceremoniously, and looked at the USGA's beleaguered lawyer without a hint of pity.

"Mr. Wolbrette, call your next witness."

He looked down at his note pad, as if searching for some inspired tactical maneuver that would overcome the undeserved obstacles the judge had thrown at his feet with her decisive but clearly erroneous rulings on the evidence. Just when Judge Bustafani appeared to be out of patience, he looked up and said in a resigned voice, "Your Honor, we rest."

Sanders was on his feet in an instant. "Judge, there is no evidence that the USGA's claims have any validity. This so-called 'confession' has not been connected to Harold Gladstone — or anyone else, for that matter. For all we know, it's a product of the overactive imagination of a young man with his own agenda."

That last comment made me almost come out of my chair. I must have made a noise, because Wolbrette turned and frowned at me.

Judge Bustafani raised her hand to cut Sanders off. "I tend to agree with you, Mr. Sanders. Without some evidence to prove that Mr. Wolbrette's note was written by Mr. Gladstone, there is nothing to support the statements the USGA intends to publish as part of its exhibition that Mr. Gladstone, not this other fellow, killed his wife."

She turned to Steve Wolbrette. "I don't like to issue preliminary injunctions. They're a headache to enforce. But Mr. Wolbrette, unless you can give me something more, the plaintiffs have made out a prima facie case for relief."

Wolbrette rose slowly, clearly searching for something to say. In an instant, I knew it was all coming to an end.

"Your Honor, we have no additional evidence. On such short notice, . . ."

"That's why it's called a preliminary injunction, Mr. Wolbrette. It is not a permanent injunction. We'll have a trial on the merits after you have conducted full discovery. If you think Mrs. Leigh's testimony is important to your case, you can locate her and take her deposition before the trial." She looked over at Sanders and arched an eyebrow. "Mr. Sanders, can we assume you will produce your missing client for a deposition?"

Sanders had no choice but to agree.

The judge's remarks made it clear that she considered her

ruling to be temporary in nature. I then understood that she wasn't cutting Wolbrette any slack because she believed he had another bite at the apple. Under ordinary circumstances, she would be right.

But these were no ordinary circumstances, and Wolbrette couldn't tell her there wasn't going to be a trial. He took one last shot.

"Your Honor, injunctive relief is extraordinary. The plaintiffs have a damage remedy if they are truly harmed. We do not believe they are entitled to suppress this information through an injunction."

Bustafani seemed to appreciate his effort. "If we were dealing with a public figure, I might agree. But Harold Gladstone was not a public figure, and neither is his family. There is no overriding public interest in the publication of this information, especially if it is not true."

She tapped at some notes in front of her with her pencil. "According to the recent case of Stanford v. Catalonia, which the plaintiffs cited in their brief, I'm compelled to grant the injunction unless someone can testify that your note was written by Harold Gladstone. So ordered."

No sooner had she finished than a timid but familiar voice was heard from the rear of the courtroom.

"I can identify the handwriting on that note."

I spun around and saw Katharine Leigh.

Chapter 29

WE HADN'T SEEN her enter the courtroom. Apparently, even the threat of alienation from her own family couldn't override Katharine Leigh's conscience.

Over Walter Sanders's protests, Judge Bustafani reopened the evidence and allowed Mrs. Leigh to testify. She identified her father's handwriting under the glares of her brothers. Clutching a handkerchief and obviously fighting back tears, Mrs. Leigh then described how she learned about the document and confirmed the circumstances under which she had given it to me.

Wolbrette kept his questions simple and asked them slowly. At one point, he poured a glass of water for her. He kept his examination as brief as possible and resisted the temptation to ask why she hadn't appeared earlier.

For the first time all day, Sanders was thrown off balance.

He stumbled through a short and ineffective cross-examination, which was necessarily awkward because the witness was technically one of his own clients. Her testimony was antagonistic to her brothers, placing Sanders squarely in a conflict of interest. Had he been thinking better, he might have persuaded the judge to recess the hearing to allow him to withdraw and have the brothers and their sister retain separate counsel. None of that occurred to him, however, as he mumbled a final "No further questions" and sat down.

As decisive as she had been in her earlier ruling, Judge Bustafani was equally direct in reversing herself. "There is positive testimony from one of the plaintiffs that the note in question was written by her father. She did not hesitate to identify his handwriting. This is an admission against interest that is entitled to great weight. Accordingly, I find that the plaintiffs have failed to sustain their burden to show that they are likely to prevail on the merits. The restraining order is dissolved, and the preliminary injunction is denied."

With that, the judge banged her gavel to indicate that court was adjourned. Brett Sullivan had me in a bear hug before I knew it, and Steve Wolbrette and I began receiving congratulations from a number of USGA staffers and Executive Committee members.

Out of the corner of my eye, I saw the Gladstone brothers staring hard at their sister, who was nervously gathering her things as she prepared to leave. I rushed over to her, fearing that she might be defenseless if they chose to confront her.

"Mrs. Leigh, you sure have an incredible sense of timing."

She managed a brave smile, but I could see that she was in a great deal of pain over the whole ordeal. "I guess I knew all along that it was the right thing to do, but it wasn't easy." Her eyes became watery. "I don't know if my brothers will ever speak to me again."

I gave her an awkward hug and said, "Maybe not, but I bet the Reverend Leigh is very proud of you right now."

She smiled again. "Thank you. I know you're right, but I guess I needed to hear someone say it."

She then asked me about Stedman's exhibition. I was pleased by her interest and introduced her to Brett Sullivan. She quizzed him about the exhibits as well and asked when he thought the displays might be open to the public. Before Mrs. Leigh left, Brett promised to send her pictures of the exhibition that she had now made possible, and I vowed to call her with a personal report on how it went.

Back at Golf House, Sullivan said to me, "I guess I can finally show you what we have worked up."

He took me down a long hallway to the new wing. We went back into a shop that looked to be a combination print shop and computer graphics operation. All of the exhibits had been placed at one end of the room.

There was more than I expected. The artwork was beautiful, and everything was presented well. It was a funny feeling to see my summer reading material from that dingy conference room brought to life so effectively.

I told Sullivan how impressed I was. He seemed genuinely pleased. "This was a real challenge for us. Whenever we've honored other great players, like Hogan or Nelson, we had all kinds of background reference material. But the whole reason for this exhibit is to create a reference source on this guy."

Sullivan pointed to a series of large posters entitled "The Beau Stedman Story." As he explained, "Instead of laying out old newspaper and magazine articles or books or pictures, we took your report and put it in a story format for everyone to read."

If Brett Sullivan wanted my imprimatur, he got it on the spot.

We spent the rest of the afternoon discussing the schedule for the exhibition. Sullivan wanted it to open in April, to coincide with the start of the golf season. He also wanted me to be there, and even suggested that the media might want to interview me about my part in bringing this to light.

I told him that April would be a critical time, right before finals, and that I doubted that I could make it then. He seemed disappointed — so much so, in fact, that he ultimately decided to move the opening back until the third week of May, after I had the last of my final examinations.

I was then given a tour of Golf House and visited with David Fay, the Executive Director, and Frank Thomas, the Technical Director who tests clubs and balls to make certain they conform with the rules. Thomas is supposedly the only person in the world who knows which ball is really longest. Try as I might, I couldn't get him to tell me which one it was. In fact, he wouldn't even answer when I just asked him which ball he played.

I was scheduled to fly out the next day. Sullivan invited me to dinner that evening. We went to a place called the Princeton Tavern, a colonial style restaurant where the food and atmosphere were both good.

I became more and more excited about the exhibition as Sullivan explained that they would run stories in the USGA's Golf Journal over the next couple of months about it. There would also be numerous press releases for consumption by the national media. In Sullivan's words, "The word is about to get out about Beau Stedman."

It's about time, I thought.

Chapter 30

MY SECOND YEAR of law school was pretty much a blur. Both semesters were filled with important courses that demanded a lot of time and attention. As a result, I had little time even to stop and take notice of how quickly the year was moving. Nonetheless, I continued to do well, even in the spring semester when I was fighting the distraction of the approaching exhibition at Golf House.

For some reason that has never been very clear to me, the only grade given for each course in law school is the grade on the final examination. No other tests are given, and no credit is awarded for class participation. For this reason, law school finals are a nerve-racking experience.

When it was all said and done, however, I had maintained my class ranking, and the best thing I could say about my second year of law school was that it was over (and that my relationship with my girlfriend Nicole had somehow survived). I had taken some very difficult courses in both semesters, and I figured there was no way my final year of law school could be nearly as tough.

My last exam was over just five days before the opening of the USGA exhibition on Beau Stedman. I planned to fly to New Jersey for the opening of the exhibition and then home to Birmingham for a week before starting my second summer at Butler & Yates.

As expected, law firm recruiting had intensified during my second year. I had a number of opportunities to spend my summer working at large law firms in New York or California, but the folks at Butler & Yates had been very good to me, and I was comfortable going back there.

Besides, Fred Nathan and I had stayed in touch during the year, and I had grown to like him more and more. He had undergone laser surgery on his eyes and was no longer in need of his thick glasses. He bragged to me that it had really elevated his golf game. He said that the thick lenses had distorted things and that he saw everything better now.

Nathan even claimed that he was now a master on the greens because he could read putts so much better. In fact, he let me know that he had recently broken 80 for the first time and was anxious to renew our golf rivalry as soon as I got settled in for my second summer.

Nathan was also impressed to learn about the USGA exhibition and even talked about going to the opening. Unfortunately, an IPO was due out the week after, which meant that he wouldn't have time to sleep that week, much less take a short vacation to Far Hills.

I arrived at Golf House the day before the exhibition was to open. Brett Sullivan gave me a sneak preview. They had done even more work and, even after having seen the layout before, the exhibits exceeded my expectations.

There was a section setting forth the story of Beau Stedman. Another exhibit showed a chronological record of his matches against everyone from Jones to Palmer. And then, of course, there was an exhibit with enlargements of Jones's notes of Stedman's scores at the "Invitational."

The exhibit attempted to explain the mystery surrounding the scores. It turned out that this was the exhibit that most intrigued the USGA staff. There had been a rather animated debate among several of the amateur historians on the staff about what the scores really meant. Although there were several interesting theories, there simply wasn't enough evidence to support one or the other.

Through computer imaging, the old faded newspaper photographs of Stedman had been enhanced. In particular, the one with him standing next to Byron Nelson, Jimmy Demaret, and Jackie Burke at Walden in Texas came out well.

Of course, the most powerful part of the exhibition consisted of the displays showing how the false murder accusation in 1930 drove Beau Stedman underground and deprived him of ever achieving his real potential in the golf world. There was a faded copy, enlarged for display, of the original life insurance policy Harold Gladstone had taken out on his wife, as well as the deed acquiring the Ocean Breakers property. And then there was the original note by Harold Gladstone admitting to the murder and proving Stedman's innocence. The cooperation of Mrs. Katharine Gladstone Leigh in bringing this to light and clearing Stedman's name was also conspicuously acknowledged.

Brett Sullivan had told me to bring my clubs when I last talked with him about my travel plans. When we finished my preview tour of the exhibit, he topped it off with a special treat: Golf at nearby Baltusrol Golf Club.

Baltusrol is one of the classic golf courses in the East. It has hosted a total of seven U.S. Opens, the earliest in 1903 and the most recent in 1993, won by Lee Janzen. It was also the site of Jack Nicklaus's fourth Open championship in 1980.

We had a perfect afternoon for golf, and Sullivan brought along two other USGA staffers to complete our foursome. We were playing the Lower Course, which was the course used for the Open. I was a little intimidated at first; not only was the course imposing, but most of the USGA staff plays to low single-digit handicaps. Sullivan said his index at the moment was 2.3; the others were under 5. After my experience at Augusta, I could no longer claim to be a 10 with a straight face. I told them I played to a 7.

We agreed to a small wager. Brett and I took on the two staffers, who worked in Championship Administration. From the looks of things, all three of my playing companions had managed to find time to work on their games. My partner knew the course well and told me how to avoid trouble. He was particularly helpful in reading the greens. We made a good team, but not quite good enough. When the smoke cleared a little over three hours later, I had lost $10 despite shooting 79.

It was late afternoon by the time we were done. Sullivan had reserved a table for dinner in the club's dining room. After a shower and change of clothes, I was hungry. My friend recommended the prime rib and a Merlot.

I don't know if it was the excitement of the day, the heavy beef, or the cigars and cognac that we indulged ourselves with after dinner, but I didn't sleep well that night. In fact, I tossed and turned so much that by morning my bed linen looked that it had come straight off the spin cycle of a washing machine. To make matters worse, I had a nightmare, familiar to law students, that I had slept through a final exam and flunked out of law school.

I had been through this before. It happened after every exam period, starting with my first year of law school. Sometimes I slept through an exam; other times I couldn't find the classroom until the test was over.

Several of my classmates reported the same dreams. So did Cheatwood. He called it the law student's version of battle fatigue.

When we talked about it one day, he told me that the law student's nightmare ranked second only to what he now called the "Van de Velde" nightmare, after the poor Frenchman who — when leading by three strokes — made triple bogey on the last hole of the British Open to lose the championship in a playoff.

I told him I had no way of knowing how that felt.

He grinned at me. "Anyone who's ever won a golf tournament does, though. Especially the first time. It doesn't matter whether it's the British Open or the Member-Guest. I remember my first win in college. Coming down 18, I was convinced that the gods of golf were gonna return any minute from a long coffee break, discover that a horrible mistake was being made, and make me play the last hole in Pee Wee Herman's body."

I tried to conjure up that image, but thankfully couldn't.

At any rate, my sleepless night made it awfully difficult to get out of bed the following morning. I felt exhausted, and two cups of coffee did nothing to shake the cobwebs that rendered me barely conscious.

As I drove to Golf House, however, the realization that I was attending Beau Stedman's coming-out party took hold and shook me from my somnolent state. I didn't think there would be much of a crowd; Far Hills is a rather out-of-the-way place. Still, there would be a few media representatives there, especially from the golf publications, and it was my hope that they would get the world to sit up and take notice of Stedman's remarkable playing record. Perhaps some particularly enterprising reporter might even interview one of Stedman's surviving victims for their impressions about the man who had beaten them while using an alias.

It was great fun to walk through the exhibition and eavesdrop on those who were viewing the various exhibits. I had lived with the Stedman story so long that I had forgotten the impact it had on me when I first discovered how cruel circumstance had hidden this phenomenal player from the world's view for over 60 years. The reactions of people as they hovered over the displays mirrored my own from the previous summer.

It still seemed incredible to think that all of this had happened in a kind of shadow world. To be sure, the golf was real enough, but until now it had been concealed from all but a fortunate few who happened to be there.

I heard someone call my name. It was Brett Sullivan. He was beaming.

"What do you think?"

"It's wonderful," I said. "Brett, I can't thank you enough. This really brings the whole story to life."

"This is just the beginning. Peter Kenyan from *Golf Digest* is here. I've known Peter for years. I called him a couple of weeks ago about this, and he loved the story. He's talked his editors into a big feature on it for next month. Pictures and all. He brought Amy Moss with him. She's one of their best photographers."

He pointed over at a tall, thin, bespectacled man standing next to a young and athletic brunette with three cameras draped around her neck. "That's them over there."

"It's amazing that this story was lost all these years in Jones's files."

I wondered what Stedman would have thought. My only regret was that I knew nothing of his family. I hoped that the publicity of the exhibition might somehow catch their attention.

At that moment, I felt someone tug at my sleeve. When I turned, I saw a short, stooped-over old man standing beside me. I remembered seeing him earlier staring quietly at one of the exhibits. Smiling up at me with a face weathered by a life spent outdoors, he looked at me and said, "Are you the young man who is responsible for all this?"

At first, I thought he was referring to Brett Sullivan. Then I understood what he meant. "Yes, sir, I am."

He held out his hand. "I'm Beauregard Stedman."

Chapter 31

IT HAD NEVER occurred to me that he might still be alive.

But there he was. As I looked at him more closely, I recognized a much older version of the wild-looking youth in the faded newspaper photographs that were on display. There wasn't any doubt; this was Beauregard Stedman.

After what seemed like a long time, I stammered, "Why aren't you dead?"

He grinned and then gave out a thin, cackling laugh. "I'm sorry if I disappointed you." Shaking my hand, he said, "I think we should talk."

We walked outside. The sun was bright, but not hot. Definitely more comfortable than New Orleans. As we strolled about the campus of Golf House, I looked at him. "I have so many questions, I don't know where to start."

"Try the beginning."

"How old are you now?"

"I was born in 1911." He then grinned mischievously, "You'll have to do the math; I quit counting birthdays several years ago."

"So you were only nineteen when Gladstone accused you of murdering his wife."

Stedman shook his head. "That was one mean son of a bitch. I knew that the minute I met him, but I needed a job bad. And she was as nice as he was mean. I never could figure out how they ever got together."

I looked at him. "I have no right to ask this, but I will anyway: Was there something going on between you and Mrs. Gladstone?"

He looked straight ahead and kept walking. There was an uncomfortable silence. Just when I thought he was going to ignore me, he turned back to me. "She was a wonderful woman. I never knew anyone quite like her. He worked her hard. Even with four kids, he forced her to do all kinds of hard work around the club just because he was too damned cheap to hire someone else to do it."

He was speaking more slowly now, measuring his words as someone would when speaking into a recorder. "I was just a kid. I tried to help her because I could see she was tired. When she would smile at me, it made me feel so wonderful. One day I kissed her. Let's just say she kissed me back."

I could tell he wasn't going to say any more on the subject. We continued to walk, and Stedman seemed lost in thought. After awhile, he spoke again.

"You know, I was the one who found her."

I remembered that the newspaper said she had been stabbed 47 times. I tried to imagine the kind of traumatic impact that would have had on a nineteen-year-old — particularly one who was in love with the victim. Even though I was one year from finishing law school and taking the bar exam, I was not a great deal older than Stedman was at the time of the murder, and I knew that the experience would have shaken me to the core.

"What did you do?"

"I thought about the children. I couldn't let them see her like this. I locked the room and ran to find Gladstone."

"I take it you didn't realize he was her killer."

He shook his head. "I didn't think about anything like that at first. But when I found him and gave him the news, he didn't act like I expected. Then I saw the gun in his hand. He pointed it at me and said that, if I was smart, I'd get the hell out of South Carolina as fast as I could. He said he was calling the police."

He paused. I could barely stand the suspense. "What did you do?"

"At first I didn't do anything. I was too stunned by what he said. Then he pointed the gun right in my face and yelled, 'I said get the hell outta here!'"

He looked off in the distance. "That's when I ran. And I've been runnin' ever since."

When he turned back to me, he was teary-eyed. "I guess I can stop hiding now. 'Course, I been hiding so long, it'll be hard to break the habit."

We walked awhile longer without saying much of anything.

He then asked me about Katharine Leigh.

"So she was the one who won the case, huh?"

"Without her, Beau, the court would have shut us down."

"Tell me what she's like."

I described her as best I could. He seemed eager to hear as much about her as possible. I supposed he was deeply grateful to her.

When I finally ran out of things to tell him about her, I asked him about Bobby Jones.

"He was the greatest man who ever lived." He tilted his head in the direction of the exhibition. "If it wasn't for him, you wouldn't never have heard of me. He made all that possible."

It took a number of people to pull this off, I thought. "What was he like?"

Stedman smiled. "Everything you'd ever want in a friend. He was the only one who knew who I was, like my only link to the real world. The only man who knew the truth, too. The man who fed my golf. When I couldn't fit in the real world, he made another world for me."

My mind raced from one question to the next, as if I was afraid he would stop talking if I stopped asking questions. "You had a close call in Texas, didn't you?"

"I thought it was over then. They hauled me to jail. I had no driver's license. I thought I was done for sure. I finally got them to let me make a collect call to Mr. Jones. They were laughing at me. One of the jailers said, 'What good do you think some lawyer in Georgia is gonna do for you here?' Fool didn't even know who Bobby Jones was. But Mr. Jones called some of his friends, and they called some of their friends. They got some justice of the peace to set bail, and Mr. Jones wired the money right away. I got out of there as fast as I could. Mr. Jones told me later that I got out just in time, 'cause they got word of that fugitive warrant in South Carolina not long after I left."

"You know, as a law student, I'm kinda surprised Bobby Jones would have deliberately skirted the law like that."

Stedman appeared to stiffen.

"What do you mean?"

"Using his influence to help you escape a fugitive warrant." I realized that I was sounding judgmental and quickly added, "Don't misunderstand me. I know what a raw deal you got. But lawyers are taught to do things a certain way, and getting around that warrant just seems a little out of character."

Stedman relaxed. "Oh, he didn't know that there was a warrant out from South Carolina. In fact, he was surprised by it. Later on, he told me he was damned glad not to know about it. He did what he did with a clear conscience."

I knew it was time to change the subject. "You beat Jones in the Southern Amateur."

"I was lucky. It doesn't matter anyway; he's still the greatest who ever lived."

I could tell he was becoming more comfortable with me. I asked him, "Why didn't you ever play him again?"

He laughed. "Oh, we played together lots of times. I had the run of the place at the National. Who do you think was the first greenkeeper there?"

It never occurred to me that Jones might have granted Stedman asylum at Augusta National. If I ever had to be placed under house arrest, it would certainly be my first choice. Augusta National would have been the ultimate gilded cage for any golfer.

"How long did you do that?"

"I never really left. At one time or another, I did just about everything there. Greenkeeper, caddie master, waiter, cleaned the cabins, too. I lived there for years. After Mr. Jones and Mr. Roberts died, though, I moved out. By that time, I had saved enough for a house in town. Been living there ever since."

It made perfect sense. Once Jones got Augusta National up and running, it was the ideal place for Stedman. He had a wonderful place to play golf away from prying eyes, and Jones always knew where to find him. No one protected its privacy like Augusta National.

"Did the other members know who you were?"

"Mr. Roberts knew the whole story. He told me not to worry. He told me just to let him know if I had any problems." He laughed. "Everyone around there was too scared of Mr. Roberts to bother with me."

I knew that Roberts ruled the club with absolute authority. They said that he controlled everything, more so than Bobby Jones.

The little man chortled. "If Mr. Roberts had been in charge of security at the White House, you'd have never heard of Monica Lewinsky."

I suddenly thought about the mysterious scores for the

"Invitational."

"One of the exhibits in there shows some scores that Mr. Jones recorded for you at something he called The Invitational. At first I thought it meant you had played in The Masters, but the scores don't match anything I could find."

Stedman laughed again. "They were from The Masters, alright."

I didn't see how that could be and said so.

"Have you ever heard of a marker?"

I still didn't catch on. "Huh?"

He explained. "Whenever the field has an odd number and someone has to play by himself, they send a player with the odd man out to record his score. It gives someone to play with, too, so he don't get out of step with the rest of the field. In the old days, they just picked a good player who could keep up. It's become such a big deal now that they got a system to select 'em. Now they're mostly amateurs who just missed getting an invitation. Every once in awhile, they let the son of a member be a marker if he's good enough."

He looked at me to make sure I understood. "Back then, I was their favorite marker. Mr. Jones loved to throw me in there because I would usually beat whoever I was playing with."

"You were shooting some great scores."

He nodded. "I should have; I was playing there all the time. No one knew that course like I did. Hell, in the early days, I set most of the pins myself."

That explained why neither Stedman's name (nor any of his aliases) ever appeared in the scoring histories that I read.

Markers' scores were not posted.

"What did the other players think?"

"Most of 'em didn't say anything. Those who did usually were nice, but some of 'em just said I was lucky. I didn't play with any of 'em more than once or twice, or they might've made more of it. They really didn't keep track of my score, anyway. Mr. Jones wanted me to keep it, though, because he was keepin' track of it."

A smile slowly spread across his face. "I'm surprised you didn't know about markers. 'Cause that's what you been doin', you know, all this time. You been markin' my card. Charley, you're my marker."

"Too bad I never got to play with you."

"It ain't required. Read Rule 6."

He had surprised me again. "Are you a rules expert, too?"

He shrugged. "If you're gonna play the game, you oughta know the rules."

Once again I marveled at the tiny man walking beside me. He had beaten virtually every great player of his day. The thought reminded me of another question.

"It's too bad that you never got to play Sam Snead or Ben Hogan."

Stedman stopped and straightened up. "Oh, I played them alright. And I beat 'em both, too."

"But I thought Snead wouldn't play you, and Hogan got sick. That's how you got to play Nelson, Demaret, and Burke that time in Houston."

"I played Snead at Augusta twice. You know, he won the

tournament three times. And it was no accident, either. He'd come in as much as two weeks early so he could get the best caddie at the club and play every day with him until the tournament. He wanted to know how every putt broke so there was no guesswork."

We had come to the end of the property and turned back. Stedman continued. "Mr. Jones must've said something to Mr. Roberts about Snead not playing me. Anyway, Mr. Roberts cornered Snead one day and bet him he couldn't beat the club's greenskeeper. No one turned down a challenge from Mr. Roberts, so Snead agreed to play me. He shot 69, but I shot 68."

"You said you played him twice."

"Yeah. Snead was so mad he wanted to play again the next day. I shot 31 on the back for a 66. Eagled both 13 and 15 that day, and beat him worse than the first time. I forget exactly what he shot that second day. Anyway, he said he was done with me after that."

"I'm surprised even Roberts could get Snead to play you. They say he always checked out his competition pretty carefully before agreeing to any match."

Stedman laughed. "Mr. Roberts decided how many practice rounds you got to play before the tournament. Snead wasn't about to risk getting cut off. They also had a rule about playing more than one ball. Frank Stranahan found out about it the hard way; Mr. Roberts jerked his invitation for breakin' the rule. Anyway, if Mr. Roberts liked you, he'd look the other way. Snead was always dropping a second ball, and I guess he was afraid they wouldn't let him do it if he didn't play me."

"Did Snead talk to you much?"

"Oh, he got pretty damned nosy when I started outdriving him. Kept asking me, 'How come I ain't ever seen you out on tour?' He'd say, 'If you're this good, why don't you come out?' I'd tell him I was happy working at Augusta. I don't know if he was ever satisfied with that, though."

He looked off for a moment. "I'll tell you one thing: He had the prettiest damn golf swing I ever saw. Still does. I never missed watching him, Mr. Nelson, and Mr. Sarazen start the tournament." He suddenly seemed sad. "I guess I thought Mr. Sarazen would never die. It's gonna be hard to imagine the tournament without him."

"You beat all three of 'em. Did they ever recognize you?"

"Naw; I didn't go near enough to 'em for that. Besides, that was a long time ago, and we've all gotten a lot older. Mr. Snead and Mr. Nelson probably wouldn't know me even if we were to speak to each other."

I was dying to know about Hogan. "How on earth did you get to play Hogan?"

"That was much later. Mr. Roberts was behind that, too. Hogan wasn't playing much tournament golf then, but he played everyday at a place in Fort Worth called Shady Oaks. I'm not sure how it came about, but Mr. Roberts sent me over there to play him sometime in the '60s. I've still got the card. Anyway, we had a helluva match. If Hogan could've putted worth a lick, he would've beaten me. By that time, he had the yips so bad I couldn't bear to watch him with a putter in his hands. He only missed one green all day, but he took 35 putts.

Shot 72. I shot 70 and beat him by two strokes."

Knowing Hogan's reputation as the "Wee Ice Mon," I asked Stedman what he was like to play with.

Stedman's tone grew serious as he recalled the man known for his steely bearing. "Before and after the round, he was very friendly. Once we teed it up though, his eyes changed temperature."

"What do you mean?"

"They went from warm to cold in a hurry."

I wondered if Hogan was as distant on the course as he was reputed to be. "What did you talk about during the round?"

Stedman gave me a sharp look. "There was no small talk. It was almost like he was in a trance. He just got so wrapped up in what he was doing. 'Bout the only thing I ever heard him talk about was his 'trajectory.' At the time, I didn't know what the hell he meant."

The old man then allowed himself a smile as he recollected that day in Fort Worth. "Not that I minded him being so quiet. I'd much rather that than the guy who plays games with you — you know, moving during your backswing, that kind of stuff."

We walked for a ways in silence as I digested what he was telling me. If he was telling the truth — and I had to believe he was — Stedman's record was even better than I had imagined. Beating Snead and Hogan completed his résumé. I chuckled to myself. And he had done virtually all of his bounty hunting while he was right under the noses of the South Carolina authorities just across the state line in Augusta. Who would've ever thought of looking for him at the National?

I asked him if he wanted to meet the media and let the world know he was still alive.

He slowly shook his head and said cautiously, "I don't know if I'm ready for that yet. I've been hidin' almost all my life. This is all a bit much. You better let me think about it."

It was clear that he was getting tired. I asked him where he was staying, and he mentioned a small motel nearby. I took him there. He declined my invitation to dinner, but agreed to talk with me again the next day. As we parted, he said, "Please tell Mrs. Leigh how grateful I am." He hesitated a moment before adding, "I'd like to meet her one day."

I went back to my hotel and postponed my flight home.

Chapter 32

I WENT TO STEDMAN'S hotel promptly the next morning, but he wasn't there. The clerk at the front desk indicated that an old man matching his description had left an hour earlier after asking for directions to the nearest golf course or practice range. The clerk then directed me to a place a couple of miles down the road.

I pulled into the parking lot of something called Flanagan's Golf Center and found Stedman at the far end of the range hitting balls. I stood and watched from a distance for several minutes. At his age, of course, he could no longer hit the ball very far. But the grace of his once-powerful swing remained. He made solid contact with the ball each time, and shot after shot flew directly at the 150-yard marker.

I felt reluctant to intrude, but I drew closer to him to get a better look. Even as I stood close by, he remained absorbed in what he was doing and repeated the same routine before each shot. He never failed to make solid contact and appeared to strike the ball in the dead center of the clubface on each swing.

Finally, he looked up and saw me. Smiling, he pointed at his club and said, "I use to hit it that far with a niblick. Now it takes one of these fancy clubs."

He was holding a metal five-wood. I started to tell him that I couldn't think of many men his age who could hit the ball as well as he did with any club, but somehow I figured he didn't want to hear that.

We sat down on a nearby bench. The accuracy of his shot-making made me curious about his game.

"Who taught you how to play?"

"No one, really. I started out as a caddie at East Lake, and I got to watch Mr. Maiden play. He was the pro there. When he gave lessons, I'd hang around and listen in as best I could. And of course I was able to see Mr. Jones play all the time. There was also a great lady golfer there. Her name was Alexa Stirling. I learned a lot watching her swing. The caddies were allowed to play real early in the morning, and I just tried to imitate what I had seen."

I asked him what he thought about when he played a shot.

"Where I want the ball to go." I guess I had expected more, but that's all he said. He gave no hint of any mechanical thought, just focusing on the target.

"How did you learn to hit it so long?"

He thought a moment. "I never tried to hit it hard. That wouldn't work. The trick is to swing through the ball to a full finish. Just let the ball get in the way."

Rather than speak, I simply nodded, hoping he would continue.

"I never saw Mr. Maiden, Mr. Jones, or Miss Stirling swing hard. But most of the members I caddied for would just lash at the ball, like they were trying to punish it. I couldn't help but notice the difference."

"When did you and Jones first meet?"

He smiled at the memory. "I started winning the caddie tournament every year, and he heard about it some way or another. He asked me to caddie for him one day. After we got out on the course, he had me hit a few shots. That started it. He snuck me out there to play with him a lot after that."

I imagined that playing Stedman provided Jones with world-class competition in his own backyard. As we talked, Stedman explained that his playing with Jones was an open secret and that, although caddies were not allowed to play with members, no one at the club was about to tell Bobby Jones that he was breaking the rules. So they looked the other way.

"You were always a good putter, too, weren't you?"

He shrugged. "Same thing. You just figure out where you want the ball to go and roll it. Mr. Jones believed you should roll the ball to the edge of the cup and let it fall in. That way, even if you missed, you had a tap-in."

I remembered reading that somewhere. "Yeah, he didn't agree with the 'never up, never in' theory."

Stedman chuckled. "One fella said to him that a putt that was short couldn't fall in the hole. Jones told him, 'I never saw one that went past the hole fall in, either.'"

"Was that your philosophy, too?"

Stedman shook his head. "Mr. Jones hated three and four-footers. He called 'em 300 calorie putts. I don't know why he hated 'em so much, 'cause he never seemed to miss any. I guess he didn't like the idea of the ball hitting the hole and not falling in because it was going too fast. I always felt that it held its line a little better if I gave it a little more juice." He paused. "That's about the only thing we ever disagreed on."

Stedman's view of golf was remarkably simple and unpolluted by complicated swing mechanics. It was probably no coincidence, I thought, that so many of the great players of his day came up as caddies rather than as privileged country club members. The caddies couldn't afford lessons and learned to play by imitation and instinct. They never became distracted or confused by swing theories or conscious mechanical thoughts.

On the other hand, the members who paid for lessons expected their instructors to share some secret about the swing that would magically transform their games. As a matter of survival, the pros had to give the members something to work on. It wouldn't do to keep the game as simple as it was.

Thus, Percy Boomer came out with his "swing in a barrel" theory, while Tommy Armour touted the pause at the top of the backswing. Everyone raced to identify a key movement in the swing that produced a controlled ball flight.

The problem, of course, was that analytical thinking, when taken out on the golf course, destroys tempo and timing. A golfer with good tempo and timing can overcome poor mechanics, but a golfer with good mechanics will not improve if he is unable to swing with rhythm. And nothing destroys tempo and timing faster than the tension induced by mechanical swing thoughts. It was ironic that many golfers would be better off avoiding lessons and playing by feel.

Stedman seemed rested and ready to leave. As he stood, he reached into his golf bag, pulled out something, and handed it to me. It was the Rules of Golf.

"What's this for?"

"Like I told you yesterday, if you're gonna play the game, you need to know the rules."

He must not have liked my expression. Giving me a sharp look, he said, "You can get into a lotta trouble playing this game. Sometimes this book'll get you out better'n any club. You better know your options before you plan your escape."

I knew that the USGA and PGA conducted clinics on rules for golf officials around the country. "Did you ever go to Rules School?"

He frowned. "Naw. All you gotta do is read that little book. Hell, it's only got 34 rules. Read one a day and you're done in about a month. How hard can that be?"

"You mentioned a rule yesterday, what was it?"

"Rule 6. It sets out your responsibilities as a player. You're supposed to get a marker to sign your card."

"You said I was your marker. Don't you have to be there to be a marker?"

He smiled. "Remember what I told you about reading the rules?"

I nodded, like a schoolchild being scolded by his teacher. In addition to his other talents, Stedman appeared to be as adroit at the Socratic method as any of my law professors at Tulane.

"See if it says anywhere in Rule 6 that the marker must be present. If you look, you'll see it says the marker 'should' check the score after each hole with the competitor and record it. It doesn't say 'shall.'" He paused a moment, then added, "It's like everything else in life; it's important to pay attention."

I felt just as chastened as if I had failed to correctly answer a question in my first-year torts class. Like so many other aspects of human endeavor, it was all about fundamentals. Stedman never got away from the basics. He was direct about all things. It kept him centered. He said I was his marker, and when I argued he showed me the rule. It was as simple as that. And it was a valuable lesson.

With that settled, we drove to a diner around the corner and had an early lunch.

He had a good appetite. I suspected that was one of the secrets to his longevity.

While we ate, I asked him if he ever wanted to do anything other than play golf. He shook his head.

"There was never anything else. Nothing else feels as good as hitting the ball in the middle of the club face. Or seeing it go where you want it to go. Being able to curve it around a tree or flip it over a bunker at a tight pin. Nothin' compares to that. Nothin'."

He took another bite of his lunch. "It's just you, your ball, and the course. Nobody else can beat you. You can only beat yourself."

"Is that why you were so good at match play?"

"I suppose. There never seemed any point in worrying about what the other fella might do. I had no control over that. Seemed to me it was best just to think about getting my ball in the hole."

Once again, I marveled at the simplicity with which he viewed the game. I couldn't count the number of times I had read an article giving complicated advice on how to handle various match play situations, all based on what the opponent was doing. It seemed to me that thinking about your opponent only served to distract you from your own game. I didn't see how spending time thinking about how an opponent was playing his next shot would help me play mine.

And that's what Stedman was telling me. The way he put it, you were much better off playing your best game regardless of how your opponent was faring. Stedman maintained his focus by eliminating thoughts of anything other than the best way to play his next stroke.

"You were willing to risk a lot to play golf. Why?"

"I had a gift. Not using it would have been a sin. If I couldn't do it one way, I had to find another."

Another simple answer.

"But you took a lot of chances doing what you did."

He looked at me. "And if I hadn't, we wouldn't be sitting here today, now would we?"

Whatever had driven every great golf champion from Old Tom Morris to Tiger Woods had driven Beau Stedman.

Maybe, I thought, it was useless to put too fine a point on it. For some players, the drive to excel was the product of an overcompensating ego, a need to elevate self-esteem by achievement. They were primarily motivated by a fear of failure. For Stedman, golf was what he did best, so it was what he should do. Like everything else, it was that simple to him.

Stedman had apparently never married. He explained that he had come close a couple of times, but never could convince himself to trust any woman with his true identity. In the end, Augusta National became his family. He told me about a waiter there named Walter Abercrombie who had worked at the club for over 30 years.

"He became Mr. Jones's right-hand man. After Mr. Jones got sick, Walter took care of him whenever he came out to the club. We both did."

He told me about others at the club, too, who had become fixtures there. Many of them had their own families, of course, and Stedman often spent holidays with them.

I asked how he was doing. He said he still went to the club almost every day. Most of the old staff, including Walter, had passed away. But he was still close to many of their children and grandchildren, and he never lacked for company.

Stedman must have sensed from my questions that I may have felt sorry for him. He was quick to assure me that he was grateful for his life.

"Don't you be sad for me. No, sirree. I got no regrets. I lived at the finest club in the world. I had the greatest player in the world for a friend. And I have family. Just 'cause I didn't bring 'em into this world don't mean I don't love them and they don't love me."

There was a slight edge to his words, and I could tell that he resented the prospect of anyone pitying him.

Referring to the exhibition, he said, "And now I have this. What more could one man expect?"

Beau Stedman made the world a simple place. As if answering his prayers, God had truly granted him the serenity to accept the things he could not change. Stedman's refusal to allow bitterness or regret to absorb his energy was probably a key to his success in golf. More importantly, it was a key to his happiness in life.

Chapter 33

THE MESSAGE LIGHT was flashing on the telephone in my hotel room when I returned. Katharine Leigh had called.

I immediately returned the call. She wanted to know how the exhibit went. I didn't know quite how I should answer her, since a large part of the exhibit revealed to the public that her father had murdered her mother.

"I think you'd be pleased" was the best I could muster. She wouldn't let me off the hook, though.

"Do you think the world will finally know the truth about Mr. Stedman?"

I didn't know if she was referring to his golf or his innocence, so I gave another vague response. "I think the story is well-told."

She pressed me for more, asking for details about what the exhibits looked like. She was particularly interested in whether there were any photographs of Stedman.

I told her about the old pictures of him at various events when he was identified by his aliases. Then I gave her the big news: "I've got better than a picture, though. I was with him today."

There was a silence.

"What do you mean?"

"I mean he's here. He's alive."

She said in a halting voice, "But you told me he was dead."

I laughed. "I thought he was. No one had heard of him or from him in years. Turns out he was at Augusta National all this time."

There was a long silence. It confused me, but something told me not to interrupt. I could almost feel an immediate change in the emotional climate at the other end of the telephone line. When she finally spoke, her voice was surprisingly weak and fragile.

"Do you think I might meet him?"

"That's funny. He asked the same thing."

She sounded surprised. "Did he really?"

"Yes, he did. He's very grateful to you for making this exhibit possible."

In a polite voice, she said, "Well, that's more credit than I deserve. You were the one who made this happen, young man."

I told her there was plenty of credit to spread around. That's when she really surprised me.

"I can be there first thing in the morning."

I hadn't expected that. But I should have known that Mrs.

Leigh was someone who was not easily deterred once she decided on a course of action. It looked like Beau Stedman was going to get his wish a lot sooner than he expected.

I told Mrs. Leigh that I would expect her at the hotel in the morning. As soon as I hung up the telephone, I called Beau.

His reaction was as curious as hers.

"She wants to meet me?"

"That's what she said. She's flying up here first thing in the morning."

After a pause, he said, "Gee, I dunno. It's kinda quick, don't you think?"

I couldn't understand his sudden shyness, so I tried to make a joke about it. "Beau, she's not comin' here to marry you. She just wants to meet you and look at the exhibit. It's only natural, don't you think?"

He mumbled something I couldn't understand. When I asked him what he said, he didn't answer. It suddenly occurred to me he might jump bail before she arrived.

"Beau, this lady chose the truth about you over her own family. She made all this possible for you. Aren't you anxious to meet her?"

He emitted a sound that was almost like a moan. "I dunno. . . I mean, I guess so. This brings back a lot of things from the past, you know."

I could tell he had begun to think about things that were long buried. It had to hurt. I said as much as I could to comfort him. By the time we hung up, he had agreed to meet us and even said he was looking forward to it. I wasn't sure he meant it, and I went to bed praying that he would show.

When I saw them together the next morning, I knew instantly why Katharine Leigh never felt Harold Gladstone's affection and why she was drawn to help clear Beau Stedman's name. I also knew why she had seemed so familiar to me from the moment I met her.

The likeness was unmistakable. Katharine Leigh was Beau Stedman's daughter.

Needless to say, the reunion of a parent and child under those circumstances is an incredible event. I started to leave, but they both asked me to stay. I guess they didn't know what to say to each other and needed someone around to mediate their first meeting.

For the longest time, they just held each other's hands and cried. Sensing I was supposed to say something, I looked at them both and asked, "How did you know?"

She finally took her eyes off him. "I came to suspect it over the years. I just never felt any connection with my father. I didn't look like him or my brothers, either. And there were things said over the years, some of them very cruel. I just never thought I'd ever get to meet him."

I turned to Beau. "Did you know?"

He looked down, as if in shame. "Yeah, I knew. And he knew, too."

He looked back at Katharine. "But I didn't know if she knew, and I didn't think it would be right for me just to appear in her life and turn it upside down. I mean, what am I gonna say? *'I'm* your real father, and I didn't kill your mother, the man you think is your father did'? So I just prayed you had a good life."

They both started crying again.

Chapter 34

WHEN WE PARTED that afternoon, we promised to stay in touch. I spoke to Beau twice during the fall semester of my senior year in law school. He wanted to let me know that I could play "the National" anytime I wanted. It was his way of inviting me to visit him.

He was clearly a happy man. He and his daughter were spending lots of time together. She hadn't yet been able to persuade him to leave Augusta, though. As he explained it, he had family ties there, too. So he visited Katharine at the beach, and she came to Augusta.

Beau was also becoming something of a celebrity, and it seemed both to amuse and bewilder him. The media coverage of the USGA exhibit had a kind of watershed effect that surprised both of us at the time, although in hindsight I should have expected as much. As for Beau, he still found it hard to understand why Sports Illustrated would send Jaime Diaz to spend four days with him or why the Golf Channel (on which he refused to appear) was producing a special program about his exploits. The USGA exhibit may have secured for Beau Stedman his rightful place in golf history, but he wasn't ready to do any commercials for American Express just yet.

He was going to have to get used to the attention, though, because his story was not going to go away. Every day brought more requests for interviews and other demands on his time. If nothing else, it made him appreciate all the years he spent hidden away in his sanctum sanctorum.

Johnny Miller narrated a feature about Beau on an NBC golf telecast and gushed about his playing record, calling his string of victories "bigger than winning the Grand Slam." Jack Nicklaus generously said in an interview that Stedman must now be mentioned in any conversation about golf's greatest players. Arnold Palmer was literally besieged with questions about what he recalled of his match over 40 years ago with the diminutive former caddie from East Lake. He allowed that he did, indeed, remember it (although of course he knew Stedman by another name) and said he would welcome the chance to visit with his old opponent again.

The intense national interest in the story prompted the USGA to run the exhibit again in its museum tent at the U.S. Open. Golf Digest and Golf magazines ran competing features in the same month on the lost playing record of Beau Stedman. Numerous golf societies were pressing him for oral histories of his era. The discovery of Beau Stedman was the biggest story to hit golf in years.

We stayed in touch with each other after Far Hills, and he seemed to value my help in sorting through the madness of it all. We even planned to get together over the Christmas holidays while I was home in Birmingham. I was going to drive over and stay with him while we played Augusta together. Katharine would be there, too.

I never got to go. During "dead week" before finals began in early December, I received a phone call from Walter Abercrombie's daughter, Dolores Smith. She told me that Stedman had just died. She said that Katharine was with him at the time. He had just returned from his morning walk, said he felt ill and wanted to lie down, and passed away. She said that Katharine had asked her to call me.

I flew to Augusta for the funeral. Katharine was teary-eyed but holding up well. She smiled when she saw me. I went up to her and gave her a hug. "I can't believe this. You guys just found each other."

"But we did find each other, Charley, that's the important thing. Dad — I was just getting used to calling him that — knew he didn't have much time left. But he went out with a bang, didn't he?"

I nodded. She went on, "And we both got some closure; I think that's what they call it these days. I know who I am now. We made good use of the time we had. Let's not have regrets."

Katharine Leigh was a lot like her father.

There must have been at least 40 mourners wearing green jackets from the Augusta National Golf Club. I knew that it was against the club's longstanding rule to wear the jackets off club premises. This uncharacteristic public display was the club's way of paying tribute to its best-kept secret.

Brett Sullivan was there, too. And, of course, I ended up meeting Stedman's extended family as well. It was obvious that they all loved him. I was comforted to know that he truly had enjoyed as good a life as he claimed.

Katharine took me back to the airport after the funeral. She told me once again how much the public recognition meant to her father at the end of his life.

I looked at her. "It may be sacrilegious to say it in this town, but he may have been the best ever — even better than Jones."

I hugged her one last time, turned and got on the plane.

On the trip home, I began to reflect on what all of this meant. I have no doubt that it may be years before I fully comprehend it. Still, I managed to figure a few things out.

Beau Stedman taught me many things in the brief time that I knew him, but none more important than focus. He successfully dealt with the harshest adversities simply by accepting them. He did not allow his misfortunes to distract him. I guess he would say that he kept his eye on the ball because that was the best way to play. I have no way of knowing where he learned it, but it certainly allowed him to take full advantage of his other gifts for the game. It also enabled him to avoid bitterness, anger, and other draining emotions that so many others routinely allow to defeat themselves.

I also learned from Stedman that what separates the best from the rest is effort more than talent. Unlike professional golfers, who get a wonderful mulligan called the Senior Tour, few of us get a real second chance to seize the opportunities that we let slip by. No matter how slight our chances, we can't win if we don't play.

For that reason, I suspect few of us will ever feel as satisfied when we start adding up our score of accomplishments in life as Beau Stedman did. He gave his best effort and took his talent as far as he could.

One of my favorite cartoons has Pogo declaring, "We have met the enemy, and he is us." Beau Stedman never became his own enemy. He never beat himself up over a bad lie, whether it was on the golf course or not. He played the ball as it lay and counted all his strokes. His score was merely the measure of what he had done that day; he never let it define what he was. Regardless of the previous day's score, he was able to approach the next day's play with the same optimism.

My favorite coach in high school was fond of saying that you can't make chicken salad out of chicken shit. He was wrong. Stedman took the worst that life handed him, dusted himself off, and never took his eyes off the prize. When he encountered an obstacle, he found another way. He may not have won championships the conventional way, but he came away perhaps the greatest champion of them all.

That earnestness of spirit was no doubt the shining feature that so attracted Bobby Jones to him despite the vast differences in their circumstances. When Stedman declared in one of his letters that he would still win his championships, "you wate and see," he spoke to the very core of Jones's being.

If anyone sacrificed to conquer his own limitations, it was Jones. So fearful of competition that he vomited before playing, Jones refused to let his own pain stop him from attaining his goals, just as he later refused to yield to a crippling and painful disease even as it destroyed him.

More than anyone, Bobby Jones appreciated Beau Stedman's spirit. More than anyone, Jones understood Stedman's refusal to blame others for his misfortunes. And more than anyone, Jones understood that Stedman embodied the spirit that makes golf the greatest game ever invented.

We may be, as some claim, a nation of whiners, self-proclaimed victims who refuse to be held accountable for our own failings. But we are also a nation that has produced more than its share of Beau Stedmans, who reject the selfsame blame-shifting that threatens to become our national pastime and choose instead to play out the life they are given one stroke at a time.

Life drove Beau Stedman underground and out of golf's major championships. So he found a way to play — and beat — golf's champions in their own backyards. Life cheated Beau Stedman out of a normal family life, so he made family out of his friends at Augusta.

Golf history will record that Beau Stedman left this world as one of its greatest champions. By any measure, he was just as successful at life. They say that great players answer a bogey with a birdie at the next hole. Beau Stedman answered every one of life's bogeys with a birdie. Some would say he finished with a course record.

I will always be glad I was able to sign his scorecard.